What the critics are saying…

Slave Gamble

"In *Slave Gamble* Zoë learns to surrender to her inner desires and her passions. This is a passionate and intense read where readers are thrust into the world of dominance and submission." *~Ansley Velarde for The Road to Romance*

"*Slave Gamble* is an enticing tale of a woman's first lesson in dominance and submission…Its sensual storyline and intriguing characters makes for a very arousing read." *~ Jennifer for Fallen Angel Reviews*

Face of Submission

"*The Face of Submission* is…a compelling, graphic story of a loving D/s relationship. Erotic and confronting, yet tender and intimate. Ms. Thompson doesn't just tease with a small taste of this sub/dom relationship, she delivers a banquet. Extremely explicit , but tempered by the strong emotional content… gives a thought-provoking insight into the intricacies of this no-so-ordinary relationship." *~ Sarma Burdeu for Ecataromance*

"…both fascinating and extremely well written, Ms. Thompson was able to anticipate readers' feelings and respond, crafting a novel of adventure, wonder, hope and healing. …a different type of story that exposes the beauty of a truly healthy BDSM relationship without the rose tinted lenses." ~ *Jacque for Fallen Angel Reviews*

Jewel Thief

"Ms. Thompson mixes BDSM elements and highly romantic moments in this powerful short story. It's an intriguing plot with a surprising twist…It turns out to be a week of self-discovery, dark desires and bittersweet surrender." ~ *Reviewed by Frauke for Mon Boudoir Review*

"…an archetypical allegory turned into a cheery individualistic little exemplum of the deserving getting what they ask for. What would the world be without karma? If BDSM erotica is your cuppa tea, then this is the whole tea trolley." ~ *Maitresse NovelSpot Romance Reviews*

Claire Thompson

SLAVES TO Love

ELLORA'S CAVE
ROMANTICA PUBLISHING

An Ellora's Cave Romantica Publication

www.ellorascave.com

Slaves to Love

ISBN # 1419952617
ALL RIGHTS RESERVED.
Slave Gamble Copyright© 2004 Claire Thompson
Face of Submission Copyright © 2004 Claire Thompson
Jewel Thief Copyright © 2005 Claire Thompson
Edited by: Mary Moran
Cover art by: Syneca

Trade paperback Publication: November, 2005

Excerpt from *Sacred Circle* Copyright © Claire Thompson, 2005

Warning:

The following material contains graphic sexual content meant for mature readers. *Slaves to Love* has been rated *E-rotic* by a minimum of three independent reviewers.

Ellora's Cave Publishing offers three levels of Romantica™ reading entertainment: S (S-ensuous), E (E-rotic), and X (X-treme).

S-*ensuous* love scenes are explicit and leave nothing to the imagination.

E-*rotic* love scenes are explicit, leave nothing to the imagination, and are high in volume per the overall word count. In addition, some E-rated titles might contain fantasy material that some readers find objectionable, such as bondage, submission, same sex encounters, forced seductions, etc. E-rated titles are the most graphic titles we carry; it is common, for instance, for an author to use words such as "fucking", "cock", "pussy", etc., within their work of literature.

X-*treme* titles differ from E-rated titles only in plot premise and storyline execution. Unlike E-rated titles, stories designated with the letter X tend to contain controversial subject matter not for the faint of heart.

Also by Claire Thompson:

Slave Castle

The Seduction of Colette

Secret Diaries

Sacred Circle

Pleasure Planet

About the author:

Claire Thompson has written numerous novels and short stories, all exploring aspects of Dominance & submission. Ms. Thompson's gentler novels seek not only to tell a story, but to come to grips with, and ultimately exalt in the true beauty and spirituality of a loving exchange of power. Her darker works press the envelope of what is erotic and what can be a sometimes dangerous slide into the world of sadomasochism. She writes about the timeless themes of sexuality and romance, with twists and curves to examine the 'darker' side of the human psyche. Ultimately Claire's work deals with the human condition, and our constant search for love and intensity of experience.

Claire welcomes mail from readers. You can write to her c/o Ellora's Cave Publishing at 1056 Home Avenue, Akron OH 44310-3502.

CONTENTS:

Slave Gamble
~11~

Face of Submission
~49~

Jewel Thief
~147~

Slave Gamble

Slave Gamble

He won me in a card game.

I know, that sounds crazy. It sounded crazy to me, too. If I hadn't had more than my share of fine champagne, I might have even slapped him in the face when he told me. But instead I stood there like an idiot, letting a stranger tell me things that should have made me blush. The odd thing was, though I'd never met him, I knew him instantly.

My stupid boyfriend, Jim, had been betting at poker, as usual. He'd been drinking copious amounts of beer too, as usual. But instead of the regular poker night with his friends from work, where the stakes involved rarely went over twenty dollars, tonight he'd found himself in a 'real' game, and was in way beyond his ken.

Amelia, my one and only truly rich friend, was throwing one of her gala bashes, complete with a veritable Who's Who list of local celebrities, wealthy business people and movers and shakers in the community. As a reporter who covered the local scene, I was familiar with a lot of them, if not personally, at least by face and name.

Amelia favored 'themes' and tonight apparently the theme was roses. Inside her lovely spacious home, everything was draped in reds, pinks, yellows and whites. There was a huge ball made entirely of roses hanging from the chandelier. The scent of the lush flowers was overpowering, rising from vases all throughout the large living and dining rooms. All the 'beautiful people' were either draped attractively over the furniture, or out in back swimming in the huge pool or soaking in the hot tub.

Jim was somewhere in the bowels of the house, at his card game, and Amelia was busy being a hostess. I had stepped out by the pool to get away from the crowd, wondering, as I usually ended up wondering when I went to these shindigs, what I was doing there.

I was smoking a cigarette and thinking about what I'd tell Amelia as I made my early 'graceful' exit. I was deciding if I felt sober enough to drive, and decided that I did. Jim, who had come with me, could find his own way home. To his own apartment. I suddenly realized, or more accurately, admitted, something which was already clearly written on the proverbial wall. Jim and I were history. We were just about to figure it out, if we hadn't already.

A deep sexy voice shook me out of my reverie.

"Nauseating habit, that."

I looked around and saw a GQ kind of guy, with dark hair and eyes. He was wearing a silk shirt, casually open at the neck, tucked into black jeans over black boots. His skin was tan, offset nicely against the pale lemon color of his shirt. He was in good shape, but not from a gym. It was the kind of long lean sinuousness that comes from skiing and playing tennis; from steering your sailboat or hiking in the Himalayas. He looked sleek and as if something was coiled inside of him. Something sexy and possibly dangerous.

In a word – he was gorgeous.

I was probably staring at him like an idiot. Pointedly, I took a long drag on my cigarette, trying to look cool and bored. It was so passé of him to criticize my smoking.

"Excuse me?" I said slowly, in my best freeze-them-in-their-tracks voice, daring him to continue.

"Smoking. It makes me sick. You'll have to quit now, you know."

"And why is that?" I asked, annoyed that this stranger, no matter how drop dead gorgeous, was harassing me about smoking; my mom and Jim did it enough.

"Because I just won you in a poker game, and I like my girls to taste sweet."

I laughed then, realizing he was just having me on. Using a very creative pickup line, I supposed. Still, I found myself intrigued, and as I mentioned, a little lacking in the judgment department, courtesy of alcohol.

"Sounds like Jim really got desperate, huh?"

"He sure did, sweetheart. And I'm here to collect on his debt." He came near and leaned in close to me. I could smell his scent, something between cinnamon, lemon and musk, as he bent down and kissed me lightly on the cheek. "You're mine, Zoë," he whispered in my ear.

This was too much. I backed away from him, ignoring the whoosh of electricity that had whipped through me when his lips touched my face. Just then I saw Jim coming outside. He was looking around, probably for me. With relief I rushed over to him. "Jim, what have you been telling this guy? He claims he won me in a poker game! What is going on?" Jim came over and hugged me. He smelled of beer and sweat. Nervous sweat.

"I know this is nuts, Zoë. I didn't think he'd win! I swear, I had the perfect hand. And I was going to win back the $2,500 I'd lost and then some—"

"$2,500! What, are you out of your fucking mind? You don't have that kind of money! Don't you know, Jim, you don't bet more than you can cover! Now you're telling me you lost $2,500? Because if you think you're going to borrow it from me, you've got another thing coming—"

Mr. Tall Dark and Handsome had come up to us. He intervened, his voice smooth and suave. I wanted to smack him; to tell him to mind his own business. Jim stepped back slightly, as the man said, "No, Jim doesn't owe me $2,500. I forgave him the debt, conditionally of course. I don't need his money. I want something else he has." He looked at me, a slow smile curving up his face, his eyes sparkling in the torches set along the poolside.

I turned to him, and said, suddenly engaging in the game, "Oh, what might that be?"

He held out his hand, smiling, and answered, "My name is David. David Turner. Jim here made a very unusual bet. He bet you, my dear. And I'm here to claim my prize."

I didn't take his hand. Instead, I pulled Jim by the arm and got him out of earshot. Any trace of a champagne high was gone, and I felt a curious knot in my stomach. "Jim, what the hell is going on? Who is this guy, and how dare you *bet* me in a card game! You can't bet something that doesn't belong to you! And, in case you haven't noticed, I'm not property! I'm a person!"

Jim was sweating, more than the warm summer night would warrant. He looked anxiously over at that David fellow, who was looking out over the pool, where several very scantily clad sweet little things were romping in the water.

I turned back to Jim, waiting for his explanation. "God, Zoë, I had too much to drink, and I wasn't thinking very clearly. He kept harping on you. Like, how gorgeous you were, and how hot, and wondering who had come in with such a babe. I was so fucking sure I had it made! I was so sure I had the winning hand, I swear to god."

"But I was $2,500 in the hole, and even if I won the hand, I'd still be out some serious bucks. So when he said, I'll see your hundred, but I have a better idea. How about a night with your gorgeous girlfriend, and we'll call it even? Well, how could I refuse? I was so sure I'd win, that it was just academic. It was a joke! I had no idea he was serious!"

Jim went on, his expression pleading, "I know it's nuts, but maybe you could humor him a little or something? Let him buy you a drink, maybe? I don't know." I didn't answer. I just stood there fuming at him. The man had tried to sell me in a card game!

He went on, his voice now a whine. "Please, Zoë. I know I'm a total jerk, but to tell you the truth, I don't know what to do! I don't have $2,500, and somehow he doesn't look like the kind of guy who will say to forget it.

"Listen, all you'd have to do is spend a couple of hours with him. What do you say? Please? I'll never ask anything of you again after this, I swear!" Then Jim did the one thing that got to me. He started to cry! The poor pathetic boy started to tear up, and he was wringing his hands. I remembered that once I had actually thought I loved the guy, and he did look so miserable standing there.

And it wasn't as if this David fellow was disgusting. He was obviously rich, and totally handsome, and apparently found me attractive! It was kind of flattering, in a sick way. I said, "All right, Jim. I'll let the man buy me a drink. But just for the record, this is the last thing you'll ask of me, because as of now, we're through."

It was as if he didn't hear the last part, or didn't care. At any rate, all he focused on was that I said I'd do it. "Oh, thank you, thank you, thank you!" he cried, catching me up in a big bear hug. "Just an evening. And you have my cell number. Just call me if you need me."

Yeah, like he'd come running to save me while I was being raped. I would say, 'Excuse me, please stop raping me a minute so I can call my useless ex-boyfriend, Jim.' I glanced over at my would-be rapist. He was looking at us now, and he smiled that slow smile again. He didn't look like a rapist. He looked like a serious babe.

Jim faded away, and I walked slowly over to the man who had won me in a bet.

"You handled that well," he remarked, grinning. "Got out of the relationship without all the usual tears and fights. And now, instead of staying at this lavish, but between us, rather dull party, you get to spend an evening with me."

"I get to, eh? Well, no offense, but you are awfully sure of yourself."

He cocked his head at me, and gave me a look that sent shivers right to my core. I hoped he hadn't noticed. Who *was* this guy? Instead of responding directly to my taunt, he said, "Have you got a car, or would you like to ride with me?"

Like I would really get into this stranger's car! "I have my own car. What did you have in mind?"

"You can follow me."

"To where? I don't really want another drink, to tell you the truth." My head was starting to ache slightly, as the champagne worked its poison through my system.

"My house. It's not far from here, actually."

"Sorry. I don't go to strange men's houses."

He gave me that look again; the one that seemed to bypass my brain and go right to my soul. "You know me already, Zoë. And I know you. I know what you want, and what you need. Poor Jim hadn't a clue. And I imagine none of your other boyfriends did either. That's why such a lovely sexy woman is still unattached at the ripe old age of twenty-eight. Am I right?"

"I'm sure I have no idea what you mean," I said haughtily, though something inside me was responding to whatever secret language he was speaking. He looked at me again, saying nothing.

Instead he began to walk away. Confused I called out, "Hey! Where're you going?"

"To my car. It's out front. You can follow me. Say your goodbyes to our lovely hostess, and meet me in the driveway. Take your time; I'll wait." I considered protesting again; refusing, but it was no contest. The man, if nothing else, had me very intrigued. And truth to tell, I didn't really think he was dangerous or would harm me if I went to his house. Something in his eyes told me I was safe.

Besides, I had Jim's cell phone number.

* * * * *

His house was every bit as imposing as Amelia's. I found my hostess, and after being forced into a few minutes of small talk with some foreign dignitary, I was able to pull her aside. "Listen, Amelia! The craziest thing has happened! My stupid boyfriend. That is, my ex-boyfriend as of tonight, made a $2,500 bet he couldn't honor, and so he told this guy he'd let him spend the evening with *me* in payment!"

"What?" Amelia, a large but beautiful woman, looked down at me in surprise. "And who is this who is so taken with you? Who would pay $2,500 for an evening with Zoë Lennon? I mean, you're a cute kid, but that seems a bit steep!" She was grinning, as if she thought I was joking.

"I'm serious, Amelia! The guy in question is someone named David Turner—"

She interrupted, her eyes growing round, "David Turner! Do you have any idea who he is? Oh my god! He wants to spend the evening with you? You are *so* lucky! I couldn't believe it when he said he'd come to my party! He always turns down my invitations. Oh, very politely of course, and always with an airtight excuse, like he's jetting off to Italy, or he has a huge merger to close, and can't get away. Very posh; very proper. Very unavailable."

She stopped a moment to take a large gulp of her wine. I was able to get in a word edgewise. "So who *is* this guy? How come I haven't heard of him? I know everybody in this town, at least by name!"

"He just moved here, from Seattle. He started his own little software company, and apparently whatever he was selling was of interest to Microsoft, because they bought him out to the tune of millions and millions of dollars!

"He doesn't like attention or publicity. It was all very hush hush when he bought the old Quimby mansion. I only know about it because I live in the neighborhood! I couldn't even get him over for a cup of tea till tonight!"

"Well," I said, impressed and further intrigued, despite myself. "That's all well and good, but this guy thinks he can just 'buy' me for the evening and—"

"Oh, lighten up, Zoë! You have no idea how lucky you are! If this guy wants to take you out, and this is his way of doing it, go for it! $2,500 is like chump change to this guy. He probably spends that much on his dry cleaning bill."

"Ok, ok," I said, wondering now if he was still waiting out front. "So he's not like some ax murderer, and I can go to his house and be safe-"

Again she cut me off. "His house! You're going to his house! Oh my god! Promise me to tell me every little detail. The furniture, the artwork. Does he have a pool? How many bedrooms; bathrooms-"

"Shut *up*, Amelia! The guy isn't going to wait all night for me. You know where I am, so if I don't reappear by tomorrow, call the police! I guess I'll go check out Mr. Eligible Bachelor, and I'll give you a full report tomorrow."

"Promise?"

"Promise."

I followed his bright red Porsche with my practical Toyota Corolla, feeling dowdy, and as a result, slightly defensive. A few miles from Amelia's we came to a large iron fence. After a second, the huge gate began to swing open, allowing us to enter a long winding drive to his house. When we pulled up into the circular drive in front of the house, he was at once at the door of my car, opening it like a gentleman, holding out his hand to assist me.

I didn't take it of course; I've been able to get out of a car by myself for some years now. His drive was cobblestone, and in my fancy party high heels, I had to step carefully. He led me up to the large imposing oak door, and using an electronic key of some sort, he pushed a few buttons and we were in.

The front hall was almost as big as my apartment, but it was warmly decorated with large fine reproductions by Klimt and Franz Marc. At least, I assume they were reproductions! The floor was marble, but with an unusual inlay of a large butterfly in yellows and golds in the center of the floor, which picked up the golds in the dresses of the willowy Klimt women.

"Welcome to my humble abode," David said, grinning. "It's too big; it's ridiculous, but my accountant convinced me that for tax purposes it makes sense. Come on back to the kitchen. I'll get you something to drink. You look thirsty."

That's funny. I wasn't thirsty until he said it. Now I realized I was parched. I followed, through large rooms, all decorated in a similar fin de siècle French style. Huge windows in each wall promised streams of sunlight during the day. I wanted to stop and admire the rooms, but David was walking quickly through, and I didn't want to get lost.

Once in the kitchen, David opened the huge stainless steel refrigerator and took out two bottles of sparkling water. He poured me a crystal goblet of water and said, "To us," lightly raising his glass in my direction.

He set his goblet down and moved in front of me, so that my back was pressing against the edge of the dark blue granite countertop. I felt my heart racing in my chest. I felt like I was in high school and the cutest boy on the football team was my prom date. I was so nervous my hand actually shook slightly, and I spilled some of the sparkling water. "Oh!" I said, dismayed, trying to set the glass down with this tall man leaning so close in to me that I could see the slight stubble of his five o'clock shadow.

Without looking, he took the glass from my hand and set it down on the counter. Leaning in, he brought his lips close to mine and kissed me. It started out sweet and chaste. Just lips touching lips. Soft lovely lips. And I admit it; it was me that actually was the first to part lips, to touch his with my tongue, to invite a lover's kiss.

He leaned further against me, taking my hands in his and lifting my arms until they rested against the counter, effectively pinning me there, and holding me in that embrace, as he continued to kiss my mouth. I was captive beneath him, and somehow that added to the thrill of that kiss. He could crush me beneath him if he chose; he could take me then and there and I wouldn't have been able to resist. I wouldn't have wanted to.

It was a lovely kiss; the kind that makes you melt, that makes you want to sink down wherever you are. I might have, too, but he was holding me up.

At last he let me go, and I kind of sighed. Then I blushed, embarrassed to have been so obvious with him. Finally, lamely, I said, "Wow. Where'd you learn to kiss like that?"

He smiled at me, and I blushed even more. Talk about a stupid remark! What was I, in high school?

"Zoë," he said, "I sense something about you."

I looked at him, not certain what he meant, but feeling somehow that this was one of those pivotal moments where my life was about to take a new direction. I didn't respond.

"You need something I doubt you've ever gotten. It's something I think I can give you."

Riddles. And yet there was that secret language again, something whispering and swirling just below my conscious. I somehow knew what he was saying, even though I didn't yet have the language for it. Still, nerves or bravado made me pipe up, "Oh, yeah right. Now you're going to tell me about your huge dick and how you can give me what I need, yeah baby." I tried to laugh, tried to sound worldly and cynical, but he didn't laugh with me.

Instead he said, "Stop that, Zoë. That false, smart-ass behavior doesn't become you. It isn't you. It's something you wear like a mask, to keep people at bay. You don't need it with me. I already know you."

I swallowed. Who *was* this guy. "Let me be more direct," he went on. As he spoke, he ran a finger lightly over my cheek. His eyes were locked on mine and I felt like I was being hypnotized. "I am what you would call a Dominant, or Dom for short. That is, I am into control. The complement to a Dom is a submissive, one who submits to the wishes and demands of her Dom. It isn't about abuse, or force. It's a lovely and consensual exchange of power, which ends up creating something greater and more spiritually compelling than any mere sexual connection ever could."

"What I sense in you, Zoë, is your submissive nature. Something in your bearing, in your demeanor, tipped me off at first. I don't know how to describe it; it's a sixth sense of mine. I can connect on some visceral level with submissive women, and I've rarely been wrong. That kiss just now; it confirmed it. You are longing to submit. To submit sexually and spiritually to someone who will understand and cherish the gift of your submission."

"I want that someone to be me. As much as you long for that; I long for what you offer, in return. I want it, freely given. I want to claim you for my own."

I stared at him. How could he be saying this? Did I have a placard advertising my sexual orientation? I had never shared anything like this with anyone. And yet, there he was, spilling long buried fantasies and secret dreams as if I'd placed a personal ad spelling it out.

How many men had I tried to 'trick' into wrestling with me, only so I could manipulate them into pinning me down? How many badly written romance novels had I bought and tried to wade through, if there was a strong man ripping the bodice of the poor bosomy woman on the cover? No one had ever tapped into this part of me before. I had kept it hidden, believing on some level that I was 'sick' and 'weak' for even entertaining the fantasy of losing control to a strong man.

David smiled at me now and said, "Do you understand what I'm saying to you?"

"I- that is, uh, I don't know what to say. I don't know what you mean." I looked away. I found suddenly that I couldn't look him in the face.

"Liar."

I blushed. He was right. I was a liar. His words had inflamed me. I felt almost dizzy with still unexplored feelings. Secret forgotten dreams came rushing to me. Not images per se, but a sense of desire, of need. The need to be taken, to be controlled. Dreams I had put away, I thought forever, because they didn't fit with my image of what it was to be an independent woman.

"I see you are fighting your demons, my angel. I will help you. You don't have to decide a thing. Just stay with me. Just for tonight. Let's explore it together. Let me take you where I sense you want to go; are longing to go."

"I want you. I want to use you and I want to test you. I want to see if you have the mettle; if you have the courage to submit. Right now, you only have one decision to make. Decide if you will stay for one night. If you don't like what happens, you are free to go. In fact, you are free to go at any time. Just say 'red light' and no matter what is happening, I will stop. And you will leave this house and go back to your safe bland little world, with your safe boring little lovers."

The challenge was apparent in his remarks, but I forgot to come up with a sassy response. I felt like someone had taken a light and shined it inside my soul. I had already made the decision. I would stay. I would see what he offered. "Yes," I managed to whisper. "I'll stay."

Leaning down, he kissed me again, this time pinning my arms behind me. I found I could barely catch my breath. At last he let me go, and I had to grip the counter behind me to keep from falling. He said softly, "There are rules, my love, to your staying. You must be willing to obey these rules, and to understand them from the outset. If you stay tonight, you obey me completely. You don't talk back. You don't question my demands. You do as you're told or suffer the consequences. Do you understand, beautiful girl?"

I felt beautiful, too. He made me feel lovely and special, and also something else. Something wanton and needy, something deeply sexual and sensual. I wanted what he offered. Slowly I nodded.

"If you plan to stay, kneel before me now." His voice was low and musical. I felt as if I were caught in his spell.

He was an enchanter and I was the innocent princess. Almost in a dream, I dropped to my knees before him.

"I will stay," I whispered again.

"Good girl," he murmured, as he ran his fingers through my hair. Then, without warning, he pulled my hair and used it to lift my face so I was looking up at him. "Zoë, you aren't mine yet. But if you please me, you will belong to me. Now get up and follow me. I'm taking you to the playroom."

I followed, in a daze. I was astounded at how he had somehow taken me over so easily. How had he known my secret needs? We walked up the stairs and down a hall. He opened a door that led to another set of stairs. We climbed these as well and came to a very nicely furnished room, with a large bed, a couch, and a long low table. I guess I was expecting some sort of dungeon; I was actually kind of disappointed. Reading my mind he said, "No whips and chains. You aren't ready for that — yet."

Yet. I considered for a moment turning around right then and running. Would he let me go? Or was he really a crazy serial killer, and I was the latest on his murder list? As I was thinking this, he leaned down, gently stroking my cheek. His look was tender. "Don't be afraid, Zoë. I won't give you more than you can handle. And remember your safe word. 'Red light' and I stop. Everything stops, and we part as friends."

"But I hope you stay. I sense something unexplored in you. Something that, if you keep shut up inside of you, will prevent you from becoming whole. As I said, I have a sense about these things, and I've rarely been wrong. Trust me. Take a chance. If nothing else, satisfy your curiosity about Dominance and submission."

Well, I was curious. No, I was beyond curious; I was captivated. Every time he said that, about something inside of me that needed exploring, I felt that weird knot in my stomach. A rush of adrenaline and a tiny voice somewhere inside of me crying, "Yes!" I had to find out what he was talking about. I wanted to see if my body, which was already very interested, knew more than my over-analytical brain.

Slowly I nodded, finally letting the net of this strange dream fully descend. He smiled, and kissed my lips, gently this time, just for a moment. Standing back, he said, "Take off your dress and your shoes."

This was said so matter-of-factly that I didn't even consider disobeying. I stepped out of my Kate Spade leather pumps and stood in my bare feet, feeling short. Because it was the middle of a hot summer, I wore no stockings. Reaching behind my back, I unzipped the little silk designer number that hid my imperfections so well. I stood there in my bra and panties, thanking my stars that I had put on the beautiful new matching lacy silk underwear I had just bought, instead of my usual utilitarian white cotton. I sucked in my belly and thrust out my breasts, hoping I was alluring, while at the same time feeling very vulnerable.

David was sitting on a low leather couch, appraising me. His eyes were like dark burning coals. I felt naked. Impulsively I wrapped my arms around my torso, feeling exposed.

"Drop your arms. Let me look at you."

I started to protest, but remembered his earlier admonition. *If you stay tonight, you must obey me completely.*

Slowly I dropped my arms, taking a deep breath. I knew men liked my body; I didn't need to be shy around this man. He was just a man; like any other.

"Get on your knees and crawl to me."

"What?" I needed a cigarette.

"You heard me. Drop."

I stood there. This was nuts. I was not going to crawl to this man. Again he spoke.

"Either you're serious and willing to submit to me for this one night, or you are not. If you are not, get your clothes and get out. If you are, drop to the ground and crawl. Now."

I stared at him, feeling my ire rise. This didn't fit in with my fantasy of beautiful princess ravished and adored by the mysterious enchanter. And yet, somehow it did. I felt heated, like I was melting inside, and it radiated from my center; from my sex. I realized I was ridiculously wet, and he hadn't even touched me.

I dropped to the ground. I felt ridiculous there on my knees. But even as my face burned in embarrassment, I knew in the part of me that was most honest and least defended, that I wanted this. Slowly I crawled to David's boot-clad feet. When I got there, he lifted a foot and put it on my head. Pressing down, he forced my forehead to touch the ground. I closed my eyes, as shocked that I was allowing this as that it was happening.

"Get used to this position, darling girl. On your knees before me, with your forehead touching the ground, and that gorgeous ass raised for whatever I choose to do to it. You are ravishingly beautiful, and smart. And you are keenly aware of your own charms. You're used to getting your way, or what you think is your way. You have too much pride. You need to be humbled. You need to learn what it is to give yourself up; to surrender yourself. I know you, even though we've just met. On some level, you already belong to me; you've always belonged to me. You were born with my name under you tongue."

I was silent, hearing what he'd just said, trying it out in my brain. Yes, we did know each other on some basic visceral level that couldn't be explained or enhanced by time and familiarity. I didn't really understand all that he was saying, nor was I sure I bought into it. But I wanted it.

David continued, "The best way I know to give you a physical taste of what I'm talking about is with a nice old-fashioned spanking. Something about a hand across bare skin; it's quite humbling, I think you'll find. So lift that perfect body of yours on up and lay across my knees."

I was still kneeling, my ass in the air, my hair obscuring my face. I felt anger fighting with desire. The image of the bodice-ripping couple on the romance novel cover was a far cry from being told to prepare for a bare-assed spanking! Instead of being artfully seduced, I was going to get a spanking, like some kind of spoiled brat! But I knew even as I argued in my head that I was going to do it. My bottom actually tingled in anticipation.

Slowly I sat up and then stood, draping myself over his strong denim-clad legs. I was still in my panties and bra, which was something at least. I knew, though, it was only a matter of time before he made me strip.

I felt his fingers, cool against my thighs, and then smoothing over the silk of my pretty cream-colored panties. Slowly he stroked and massaged me through the silk. It felt very nice actually, and I started to relax.

He put one hand on the small of my back and said, "I'm going to spank you now, sweet one. Not because I am punishing you for anything. But because this will be your first taste of submission. To take a spanking, at the hands of your master. To taste pain, and feel its power. To take what I give you, and see what you're made of." *Master*. He'd come out and said it. And if there was a master, there was also a slave. A spasm of fear shot through me, like hot ice filling my veins.

I could have gotten up at that moment. I could have said that silly phrase, *red light*, and put my dress back on, and left. I was sure he wouldn't hold me there against my will. That wasn't what he was about.

But I didn't get up. Instead, I held my breath; I didn't move. I wanted to see what I was made of too. Would I like it? Would I hate it? Would I feel ridiculous and humiliated? I didn't have long to wait, because suddenly I heard a loud slapping sound. A fraction of a second later I felt a slight sting.

His hand was big, and it covered one whole cheek. The silky fabric was no protection. Again the hand came down, on the other cheek. I jerked against him. He smacked my bottom several more times. It tingled and I could feel the heat, but it wasn't so bad. I could take this! It was exciting, to be held down by the hand on my back, and smacked. My pussy was pressed against his thigh with each stroke, making me even hotter and wetter, if that was possible.

With one move, he pulled the panties down, baring my bottom. I squirmed and tried to get up. I had known it was a matter of time before I would be naked in front of this man, but when it happened, I wasn't ready. He held me down, pressing my head behind his knees, and gripping me between the couch and his body so that I couldn't move. I struggled a moment, but he was very strong.

"Stop," he said, his voice soft but steely. "Don't resist me like that. Remember who you are. This is what you want; what you need. Take it. Take it for me. You are lovely. Don't be shy about this perfect body, Zoë. You were born to be naked. I will always keep you naked, once you belong to me."

The words reverberated through me. *Once you belong to me.* This man was laying a claim to me, and he'd only known me a few hours. And yet, something inside of me responded, though I didn't say anything aloud. I was distracted from his words by his hand.

He began to spank me again, this time not stopping until my poor bottom was burning. I was struggling even though I wanted to be still. I couldn't help it. As I struggled he flipped me over, so I was balanced now on my lower back against his knees. Pressing a hand between my legs, he forced them apart.

Laughing in a low sexy way, he said, "Oh, my little slut. You are so wet. I was right. You need this. And it's just the beginning. Just the beginning." Then his heavenly fingers parted my cleft, and he slid one finger deep inside of me. I moaned and lifted myself to take him further into me. He withdrew the finger and slid it up to my clit, touching me with butterfly-light strokes. I moaned, low and guttural.

My brain tried to be embarrassed. It tried to get me to close my legs and sit up and demand my panties back. But my body overrode my brain, and I spread my legs further, wanting to feel his cock inside of me, his mouth once again on mine.

David stood up, moving so that he eased me onto the couch. He unclasped my bra, and briefly cupped my breasts in his hands. Kneeling next to me on the couch, he leaned over and licked a nipple. It stiffened and distended. He licked the other nipple, and then bit it, gently. Again I moaned, and my hand slid down to my pussy.

He grabbed my hand and said, "No. That's not yours anymore. You don't touch it unless I tell you to." He stood and pulled me up, naked. I barely came to his chest in my bare feet.

"How are you, baby?" he asked now. "Is this want you want? Are you ready for more?"

"Yes," I whispered. I usually never even kissed on the first date, but it was as if that was the 'old' Zoë. The 'fake' Zoë, even. The one who behaved the way I thought a 'good girl' should behave. Was this the 'real' me? Standing naked, breathless, flushed, longing for this man I had just met to take me, to fuck me, to, as he said, claim me?

It felt real. More real than anything in my life to that moment.

David led me to the center of the room. I noticed now that there were large eyehooks embedded in the ceiling, like you might hang a plant from. "Stay there; don't move," he ordered.

Going to a sideboard, he took out several things and came back to me. "Hold out your wrists." I did, and he put soft leather cuffs on each wrist, securing the leather over a little metal ring. He then attached a clip to each ring. Lifting my hands, he took the clips and attached them to each other. I was effectively handcuffed, my hands locked together in front of me, but in soft leather manacles.

My heart was pounding a little tattoo against my ribcage. David came behind me and caressed my hair, kissing my neck. I could feel his erection against my back. I twisted my head back to receive another kiss, and he obliged.

Pulling away from me, he said, "I'm going to secure your wrists to a chain, and secure the chain to the ceiling. You are going to let me do this, aren't you, angel?"

Still recovering from that last deep kiss, standing naked and shackled, I nodded. He took a long thin chain and clipped my cuffs to it. Then, taking a little stepladder, he climbed up, holding the chain, and secured it to one of the eyehooks. He pulled it taut, forcing my arms up over my head, fully extended.

I felt extremely vulnerable, and helpless, but also deeply aroused. He went back to the sideboard and this time he brought over a heavy flogger, dark brown suede, with a thick bundle of tresses dangling from a long thick handle. I gasped, having never seen such a thing in real life.

"It's a whip. A flogger. It's a lovely way to initiate a submissive, because its kiss can be soft and caressing," as he spoke, he dragged the tresses sensually across my back and ass, "or," and now he struck me, not hard, but hard enough to sting, "or it can bite." I jerked forward, and he wrapped an arm around my waist from the back, pulling me against him.

Kissing my hair, nuzzling my neck he said, "I'm going to whip you, Zoë. Do you think you can handle it?"

I was breathing hard, so excited I felt dizzy, almost nauseated. I tried to answer honestly, "God, David, I don't know! I never even knew I wanted this until you told me.

Well, that isn't true exactly. I mean, I've had fantasies, but I had no idea I would feel affected like this! I'm not sure I can handle this! I mean, being tied up like this, so helpless, so out of control."

"Ah, but that is precisely the point, my love. You have no control. I am simply teaching you that. Showing you what you are capable of. This is but the first taste of many wonderful adventures I foresee for us. If you're willing. But you have to be willing. This has to be what you want."

I looked at him, now standing in front of me, his expression serious, his dark eyes like a summer night, full of promise. Did I want it? Did I want to be whipped? I honestly couldn't answer the question. It was beyond my realm of experience, even in fantasy.

And yet the spanking wasn't something I'd fantasized about either. When I did allow myself to linger over submissive dreams, they were vague unformed ideas, involving harems of lovely captives, dancing in gauzy silks for their lords and masters, and then chosen as sex toys, ravished by gorgeous young princes who also pampered and adored them.

But that spanking – the physical contact, the feeling of his hard palm against my ass, even though it hurt, maybe partially *because* it hurt, had aroused me to a fever pitch.

David, so far, had been right on target about who I was, and what I needed. Could I trust him again? Should I? Was that what this was about, as much as anything? Trust? These thoughts swirling in my head as he dragged the soft suede tresses over my breasts and belly. It made me shiver, whether with desire or fear, or some combination, I couldn't say.

"And if I want to stop? If I want you to stop?"

"I'll stop when I decide it's time to stop. You can beg all you like, but I should tell you now, I won't stop until I'm ready. Of course, how you respond, what I think you can take, will be a part of what goes into my decision, naturally. But I won't stop at your command. Unless, of course, you use your safe word."

"And then you'll stop the whipping?"

"Yes, I'll stop at once. I'll stop everything. And you will get dressed, and I will walk you to your car, and maybe someday our paths will cross. And hopefully you'll remember me as a friend. And that will be that."

So, there it was. If I didn't 'submit' to this whipping, I'd lose David altogether. I'd lose those impassioned kisses, and the amazing way he made me feel – at once beautiful, wildly powerful, and also captive and under his delicious spell. I didn't want to lose all that. Who was he to make all the rules? To set the parameters of our relationship, if that was what it was, without asking me a word about it?

As if he were speaking inside my head, I heard him say that that was precisely the point. If we were to have a relationship, those would be its parameters. David as master, and Zoë as slave. David calling the shots, setting the rules, and claiming his lover. My heart was pounding as I contemplated my situation.

And yet, as he leaned against me now, murmuring my name, his cock hard and clearly visible in his pants, it was obvious that I too wielded the power. As he had said, it was a loving exchange of power. I wasn't giving myself up to him, I was giving myself over to his loving control, and he in turn was giving himself to me.

Did I want the whipping? I honestly didn't know. But I wanted what he seemed to be offering, and so I said finally, "I want it."

"You want what, Zoë? Say it."

"I want you to whip me."

"Lovely," he murmured. Standing in front of me, slowly he unbuttoned that pale yellow silky shirt. He was long and lean, but well muscled, especially his chest and shoulders. He was tanned and his stomach was strong. My eyes were drawn down to his jeans, which he didn't remove, though I was silently willing him to. I eyed the still-erect cock pressing against the denim and my mouth actually watered.

I wanted to taste that cock, but apparently that wasn't in the cards. At least not yet. Instead David said, "Zoë, I want you to really luxuriate in the sensations this whipping is going to create for you. And so I am going to blindfold you. It will heighten the sensations. Is that all right?"

I nodded, thinking perhaps that would be easier in some ways. He slipped a little sleep mask over my eyes. Now I couldn't see, and my hearing seemed to sharpen. I could hear the swish of the leather as he stroked it across my back and breasts. I could hear his breathing, low and sweet, and my own breathing, now ragged and shallow.

This was really happening! I was bound, naked and helpless in this mysterious man's house. Amelia was the only other person that knew where I was, but even so, what could she do now? She was busy hosting her gala, waiting for my call tomorrow to tell her about his bathrooms and square footage. He could kill me now, and no one would be able to do a thing about it.

This was silly! I knew I could trust David. I had known it really from the first time he spoke to me; from the first time I had felt the undercurrent of our special connection. Something about being blindfolded though, made me feel so vulnerable.

I heard the whistle a second before I felt the lash. The caressing had stopped, and the stinging began. Because I couldn't see, I never knew where it was going to land. He struck my ass first, the fleshiest part. Several times he did that, and the sting was mounting on a bottom already tender from the earlier spanking.

I started to breathe heavier now, and move in my bonds, as if I could get away. The lash landed on my thighs, and then my back. I yelped. It hurt much more on my back, which wasn't padded like my bottom. He covered it evenly, until my entire back was stinging, and I was writhing and moaning, pulling hard against the wrist cuffs.

I was whimpering, and breathing so hard I thought I would pass out. "David," I cried out, though I couldn't seem to finish the sentence, or even have a coherent thought. I was falling into some kind of ethereal realm. I felt light-headed and somehow disconnected from reality. And yet somewhere below it all I felt peaceful, deeply peaceful. But still with that burning, aching overlay of unrequited desire.

I felt his arms go around me, and his long hard body press against mine. His chest felt lovely against my breasts. I pushed into him, wanting him to take me down; to take me to his bed. "David," I begged again, still not articulating my desperate need.

"Shh," he whispered, smoothing my hair from my face, holding me in his arms. "Zoë, Zoë, slow your breathing. Calm down, baby. It's me, David. I know you don't know me yet, sweetheart. Not in terms of years. But you and I know each other. In every way that counts. Trust me, angel. I won't take you further than you can go. And if I do, you know the magic words."

Right. The 'magic words' – *red light*. I found I had no desire to say them. I was still frightened, but also deeply, almost hypnotically aroused. I felt I would do anything for him at that moment; take anything for him. He continued to hold me, and I felt my breathing slow, my body relax.

I leaned back into him. Slowly he let me go, leaving me tethered and chained. I was still afraid, but I didn't want to say those words. Not yet. Maybe just knowing that I could was enough. There was a way out, if I needed it.

He whipped me for a few minutes. Or was it a few hours? Time lost meaning, and I found myself in some kind of altered state of conscious, swaying in the bonds. I felt him releasing the chain, and then removing the cuffs. My arms fell lifeless, but he was there, holding me, wrapping me in a close embrace.

He removed the blindfold, and I had to squint to see, even though the room was dimly lit by brushed silver sconces placed discreetly along the walls. David kissed me, and said, "You were spectacular. You were born to this. You were amazing."

I smiled, and realized my body was bathed in sweat. Suddenly I felt cold, as the sweat began to dry. David scooped me up in his arms and carried me from the room.

Down the hall we came to his bedroom. Kicking the door open, he brought me into a huge room. The large bed was set in a black iron frame, with little stars and moons artfully wrought at the headboard and footboard. Gently David lay me down on soft satin covers. I watched quietly as he took off his jeans, and peeled down his underwear.

His body was beautiful; an athlete's body, with those sweet little indentations below each hip. His cock was erect, and again my mouth watered as I looked at it, now naked and ready, I hoped, for my kisses. He approached me and climbed onto the bed.

We kissed for a few moments, and then he straddled my chest, pointing his cock at my lips. I parted them, wanting to take him in my mouth. To feel his hardness swell against my tongue. I licked the head, teasing him, slowly licking down the shaft, and back up again, until he lost patience and pressed himself into me, moaning with pleasure.

I used all my skill to kiss that beautiful cock. And now it was clearly the 'slave' in control of the 'master', as I wrenched moans of pleasure from his lips, and made his body twist and arch in pleasure.

He pulled away, his eyes bright, his voice hoarse with desire. "God, Zoë. I have to fuck you. I have to have you." He leaned down over me, balancing himself on his elbows as he moved himself so that his cock was right at my entrance. I arched up, urging him with my body to take what was his; what had always been his.

He stretched himself across me, covering me, and pulled my arms up, holding my wrists high above my head, trapping me again, making me feel helpless and wildly wanton at the same time.

When he finally entered me, I came almost immediately, writhing and pushing against him, trying to take him further into me, wanting to possess him in this most primal of ways. He obliged, thrusting hard into me, forcing an unladylike grunt from me.

Then, in a steady lovely rhythm, he moved in and out of me, and again the hot roiling pleasure boiled up in my belly, as his cock filled me, and his movements created perfect friction against my distended clit. Still he held my wrists against the pillows, and somehow that only added to my fierce pleasure. The sensations became overwhelming, and I heard a thin keening sound, which it took me a moment to realize was me.

David bucked, dropping my wrists now as he wrapped me in a tight embrace. Softly he cried my name, "Zoë, Zoë, Zoë," hiding his face in my neck as he came, pushing and pumping into me as if his life depended on it.

Then he collapsed, and I could feel his heart thrumming and crashing against my own. We must have fallen asleep, because I woke up sometime in the early dawn. David was sleeping next to me, and we were both under the sheets, which were of the softest imaginable cotton.

I felt a desperate need for a cigarette, but I didn't feel like moving. I looked over at this amazing man who had boldly entered my life on a bet, winning me in a card game! He looked younger asleep. Vulnerable and innocent. I felt a welling up of great tenderness toward him. Yes, he was still gorgeous and no doubt, the minute he woke up, once again very much in command.

But now I leaned over and kissed his forehead. He stirred slightly, but didn't waken. Finally my bladder got the best of me, and I slid out of the bed, looking for something to put on. I found a big terry cloth robe. It was miles too big, which made me feel small and feminine.

The master bathroom was just off the bedroom, complete with a huge sunken tub, a shower, two sinks, two toilets and a bidet. For now I just used the toilet, then splashed water on my face, and went in search of my purse. Nicotine was calling.

I found it where I had dropped it, in the lovely front hall with the curious butterfly. Inside was a package of Newport Lights. A further search yielded a lighter. I almost opened the front door, but I saw the little telltale light on the alarm box near it and realized I might set it off.

Damn! I would have to wake him. I went back and shook David's shoulder gently. "David! David, wake up. I'm sorry to bother you, but I really need a smoke. I didn't want to trip the alarm."

David opened one eye and squinted sleepily at me. "Zoë?" Then he smiled, like maybe he had thought at first I was a dream, and was pleased to see me in the flesh. "Zoë, it isn't even light out yet! Come back to bed. You can have your fucking cigarette when we wake up."

But now I was determined. My habit was stronger than my consideration. "Come on, David, just tell me the code. I'll go out by myself."

David sat up, now looking fully awake. "Hey, that's my robe. Take it off."

"What?"

"You heard me. I want you naked, unless I tell you to put something on. Do it." Slowly I slipped the robe from my shoulders, feeling the beginnings of that strange hypnosis fall over me again. What spell did he have, to control me like this?

"That's better," he smiled, looking at my breasts, and further down, until I blushed and turned away. "You can have your cigarette, though I should warn you you'll be quitting, now that you're with me."

"Well," I said laughing, "maybe you'll have better luck than I've had! I've tried to quit like five times so far, and it hasn't worked."

"That's because you didn't have me, darling," he grinned, cocky as usual. He got up, putting on the robe I'd discarded, and led me to a room that opened out onto a private veranda, after punching a few numbers into the little alarm box by the door.

"Come on," he said, "no one can see you. I want you naked here. Though, you know, eventually you'll be naked other places. Places that aren't private. And you'll obey me then too. You know why, angel?"

"Why," I whispered, joining him on the veranda as the sun spilled up over the edge of the mountains. The air was cool and pleasant, but already hinted at the hot summer day to come.

"Because that's what I want. And you want what I want, don't you, Zoë?"

"Yes," I breathed, meaning it. To my surprise, the aching desire for a cigarette had given way to an aching desire for him! Instead of lighting up, as I had planned, I dropped to my knees in front of David and opened the front of his robe.

I looked up at him, silently asking permission to give homage to his beautiful member. He nodded slowly, a smile stealing across his face. I took his cock, only half-erect, into my mouth, and massaged it with my tongue and lips, feeling the heat of it as it expanded and lengthened against me.

David sighed, and let me kiss him for a while. Then he pulled away, lifting me up. "Come back inside, Zoë. Do you still want that cigarette?" I shook my head, marveling that it was true.

We went back into the bedroom, and into the bathroom, where David peed, completely at ease in front of me, as if we'd been lovers for years instead of one night. He brushed his teeth and then said, "Well, it's only five o'clock, but I'm awake now. How about you? Breakfast in bed? Or would you rather eat in the kitchen? My cook won't be here until 7:30. That's when I usually eat, you see."

"Your cook!" I was impressed, though not surprised, given his obviously lavish lifestyle.

"Yes," he said, as if this were a common thing. "She can make us another breakfast later. I have a feeling we'll be hungry," he grinned conspiratorially. "But for now, how about some coffee cake and a cup of strong java?"

It sounded good to me, and I followed him into the kitchen, still naked, and wishing I had a wrap. As he made the coffee, grounding the fresh beans in a little machine on the counter, I got up the nerve to say, "David, I'm kind of cold. Do you think I could wear a robe?"

He looked at me, first my face, then slowly, up and down my body. "No, sweetheart. I'm sorry, but I like you naked. At least for now. I love the look of your skin, so ripe and soft, like a perfect peach. I love the way your breast rest, high and round against your narrow ribcage. I love that tapering waist and that cute little bellybutton."

I was blushing now, embarrassed but pleased at his lavish praise and obviously sincere appreciation. But then he threw me for a loop. "This, however," he said, leaning down and cupping my pubic curls, "I think this has to go. I want to shave you. Shave your pussy. I want you bared for me. And I think you'll find it heightens all sensations."

I stared at him, my eyes wide with surprise and disbelief. He must have seen the hesitation in my face, because David said, "Don't say no, darling. Remember, that isn't your prerogative any longer. You belong to me now. We both know it. But I want to hear you say it. To admit, and to accept what and who you are. And so I'll ask you now, who do you belong to, Zoë?"

There it was again, his hypnotic voice, low and pleasing, somehow entering inside of my very essence to claim me. I found myself answering, "You, David. I belong to you."

"That's right, angel. And I want to shave your pussy, and you'll let me, won't you?"

Again I nodded. David smiled, and said, "But first coffee! You wouldn't want my fingers to slip from lack of alertness, would you now?" Indeed I didn't! We drank the coffee, delicious with fresh cream and a hint of cinnamon. David had some cake too, but I found I was too nervous to eat, now anticipating a cold razor, held by someone else, scraping along my most private and sensitive parts.

I couldn't believe on one level that I was even contemplating it, but as we sat together at the long bar, sipping our hot coffee, it seemed almost natural. Of course I'd shave for my master, if that was what he wanted. My master! The words slipped into my mind unbidden, but once said, couldn't be unsaid.

When he was done, we walked together back to the bathroom. David turned on the water in the big tub. It filled quickly, and he added some sweet smelling oils to it as the steam rose invitingly.

While waiting for the level to rise, David said, "First we'll cut off the excess hair. That will make shaving much easier." He knelt in front of me with a long pair of barber scissors. I felt a little nervous having a pair of scissors so close to my pussy, but I trusted David.

Gripping my pubic hair, he snipped and cut until it was as short as possible without shaving. I felt very strange, but also aroused, which seemed to be my constant state around this man.

Once the tub was full, David got in first, and held out his hand to me. I stepped in and nestled back against him, feeling his warm hard body, settling into it like some human chair. He held me for a while, and then said, "I think you're ready. Sit up there, on the ledge. Spread your legs for me, and stay very still. I don't want to nick you."

"David," I began, suddenly unsure again, but he stilled me with a touch of his fingers to my lips.

"Zoë. This is what I want. Don't defy me on this. This is what I want. Isn't that enough for you?" Yes. As crazy as that sounds to someone who doesn't understand the Dominant/submissive relationship, it *was* enough. More than enough.

I spread my legs and sat very still as he smeared extra baby oil across my mons and labia. Then, taking a fresh razor, he slowly drew it first across the top and then lower, over the delicate labial folds. He did this over and over until I was as smooth as a baby. "Stand up," he commanded, "and look at yourself."

I did as he ordered, and was surprised to see, not the features of a little girl as I'd expected, but a grown woman, with the inner labia peeking alluringly from the center. It was very erotic somehow, and I felt myself swelling with desire.

"You're beautiful like that, Zoë. I'm going to keep you like that. You have a perfect cunt. Now sit down. Let me taste you." I sat on the little ledge again, and David knelt up in the water, and put his face to my now nude pussy.

I felt his tongue lightly against my sex, and I spread my legs, wanting more. I let my head fall back and my eyes closed in pleasure as I felt his warm velvet mouth suckle and tease me. He licked and kissed me, keeping my legs spread wide with his strong hands on my thighs, until I felt the delicious impending release of a very strong orgasm weaving its way through every nerve of my body.

It caught me suddenly, as he held me, his mouth hot and perfect against me. I jerked, but he held me tight, and continued his kisses until I was shuddering and arching against him, completely out of control. When at last my orgasm subsided, he pulled me back down into the warm water and held me against him.

"Now who belongs to whom?" he whispered, and I understood in that instance that when love is involved, there is no real line between master and slave, between owner and owned. He belonged to me as much as I belonged to him.

Face of Submission

Chapter One

Kate stood back, appraising her efforts. She would just move that one flower to better show its new blossom. Perfect. The snapdragons peeked behind stargazer lilies and Fuji mums, in a blaze of yellows and purples, accented with pink. She added a few sprigs of dark green leaves and smiled, admiring the flowers she had placed in a fine crystal vase.

Kevin would like the arrangement. He often told her how much he loved the way she kept their house. His house really, though from the moment she moved in, he'd always referred to everything as "ours". Kate had moved in two months ago, when neither could any longer deny what they shared was more than a casual affair.

Kate idly twisted the leather cuff around one wrist as she contemplated what to prepare for Kevin's dinner when he returned that evening. The remains of their French toast with strawberries was in the sink, but there was still hot coffee in the pot, and Kate would have several more cups over the course of the morning, as she straightened the house and cleaned the kitchen.

This house had become her world. Though at first she thought she would, Kate found that she didn't miss the career in publishing she had left behind. She was in the publicity end of the business, pushing the authors to the media, setting up the book tours and the guest appearances on the morning shows.

It was a hectic, fast-paced life, one that had never really suited her quiet nature. The money was decent, but the work was demanding, and her boss rode her hard to get their authors into the spotlight. Ten hours was a typical workday, and when she finally made it home to her cramped city apartment, she rarely had the energy to do much more than eat something from the microwave and collapse into bed with a good book. Her favorites were the romances, the ones with a touch of danger for the heroine.

She would find herself fantasizing that she was the one who was abducted while on a train in Istanbul, or held hostage by the handsome but dangerous desperado. Kate would fantasize about these strong but dangerous men, placing herself firmly in the story, once the book had dropped from her fingers.

Her hand would drop to her pussy as scenes of sexual torture unfolded, always overlain with a sweet romance by the end of the story. Kate was aware of her submissive nature, of her desire to yield sexually to a man. She hadn't done much by way of finding such a man in real life, however. She went out, casually, with various men who were more friends than lovers. Something in her was waiting. Like the heroines in her romance novels, she believed that someday, she would find "the one".

When her friend Amy casually announced that she was going to a BDSM play party, and invited Kate along "for the ride" as she put it, Kate was at first shocked, and then very intrigued.

"A play party? Bondage and discipline? Sadomasochism?" Kate had demanded breathlessly, as the two young women sat over Caesar salads and white wine one evening at a local restaurant.

"Yes, that's what the initials stand for," Amy said, grinning. She was the "experienced" one of the two friends, regularly attending wild parties, and invariably going home with or bringing back some young man or two for all-night escapades.

Kate admired Amy on one level—her willingness to take risks, and her complete confidence in her ability to get any guy she set her eye on. But it really wasn't Kate's style. She didn't like one-night stands, believing that romance had to play a part in things. A big cock and willing partner were just not enough, even if the guy promised to bring handcuffs and a riding crop, two of Amy's stock pieces of equipment.

Still, the party sounded fun, and it was being given in the home of one of Amy's very wealthy acquaintances, complete with flowing champagne and, in Amy's words, all the whips and chains you could want. While Kate had never been outspoken about her own submissive leanings, Amy was very vocal about her passion for bondage, and the thrill of being tied down by a lover.

Kate had come to realize that Amy wasn't submissive, strictly speaking. She was more of a pure masochist, delighting in the thrill of being bound and soundly spanked before she was soundly fucked.

Still, just finding someone willing to discuss the whole idea of Dominance and submission had been compelling to Kate, and so the two women, who probably wouldn't have been friends otherwise, met from time to time to share erotic stories. Well, mostly Amy shared and Kate listened, but this suited her.

That party had changed her life, she thought now, as she brushed idly at a sticky spot on her bare back. She would shower later, after she cleaned. The stickiness was from syrup. Kevin hadn't been able to resist her pouting little pussy that morning. As she had poured his coffee, his hand had strayed down to her shaven mons, as it often did. "Oh, baby," he had laughed. "You feel good enough to eat. Here, get up on the table, slave! I want to go to work with pussy on my lips!"

"Kevin!" she had laughed, sure at first he was teasing. But in fact, he was serious. He had Kate lean back against the table, her bottom resting lightly against it, as she steadied herself on spread legs in front of him. Kevin pushed back his chair and knelt in front of the beauty, sliding his long tongue out. He licked and teased her, bringing her to a quick but intense orgasm. He loved to hear her little moans and cries; he loved to drive her over the edge.

That wasn't the only morning Kevin had been seized with the urge to taste his lover's nectar at the breakfast table, but too often he took a deliberate pleasure from denying her release. "I want you to stay hot for me all day," he would say, while she writhed, desperate to come. He would pull away, wiping his mouth, his eyes dancing with sadistic mirth.

"Oh, please," she would shamelessly beg. "Please, Kevin! I'll still be hot for you later, I promise. Please! Just let me have one teeny tiny orgasm! Please!" But he would laugh, cupping her hot, wet pussy in his palm, and shake his head. His cock would be straining against his pants, but he would remain steadfast.

"No, no. I have to wait, and so will you. I might call you later though, and let you come for me on the phone. But be careful; don't forget Nancy's tendency to 'accidentally' listen in!" Nancy was his secretary, a woman in her fifties who Kate had met at a staff party. Nancy had looked Kate carefully up and down, a faint disapproval registering in her face before she forced a pleasant smile for the boss' new girlfriend.

Kate flushed, remembering the forbidding Nancy, and her penchant for eavesdropping. Kate recalled the time Nancy's eavesdropping had given her an earful! Kevin had made one of his teasing calls, talking softly and seductively into the phone.

He'd called her at about 10:30. Kate had almost missed the call because of the noise of the vacuum, but had caught it in time. She was breathless when she got the phone, and Kevin teased her that she'd been doing something she shouldn't.

When she'd earnestly protested, he'd laughed gently, assuring her he was teasing. "But," he said, his voice lowering, "that's what I want right now. I want you to come for me, on the phone. Where are you?"

"In the bedroom. I was vacuuming."

"Perfect. Lie down. But not on the bed. I want you on the floor." Kate did as he ordered, her pussy already wet in anticipation. Just the added idea of being forced to make herself come on the floor, like an animal in heat, had a debasing, delicious appeal to Kate. Kevin had a way of making her feel on fire with lust. She became pure sex, losing her reason as she succumbed to his dominant commands. Kate felt that Kevin had an innate understanding of the workings of the submissive mind. She had yet to realize just how true this was.

Dutifully she lay down, spreading her legs, her fingers already finding their target. "Fuck yourself for me, Katie. Make yourself come. And let me hear it. I want to hear you come, baby. Do it. Get Fatty, why don't you? Let's do this right."

"Fatty" was their nickname for Kate's battery-operated dildo. It wasn't especially long, but it was quite thick, and made of soft, pliable rubber. Kate loved the feel of it when she slid it into herself. It wasn't as good as the real thing, of course, but it was better than nothing! Especially when she flicked the switch at the base and it hummed into throbbing action.

She didn't need any more prompting. Opening her nightstand drawer, Kate took "Fatty" from the little silk bag she kept it in and lay back down, pressing the tip against her already moistening slit. Realizing she needed a little extra lubrication, Kate licked the rubber shaft, and then placed it again at her pussy, slowly pressing it in before she flicked the switch.

"Is it in, darling?" Kevin asked. She could hear that he, too, was slightly breathless and she wondered if his hand was in his pants, his back toward his closed office door.

"Yes, oh yes!" Kate affirmed, as she turned on the little motor and felt the vibrations pulsing inside of her. She moved the dildo in and out, moaning loudly. At first she was doing it "for show", to make Kevin happy and show him how aroused she was. But then she forgot the show. She barely remembered the phone, lodged between neck and shoulder, as she rubbed herself with one hand, and fucked herself with the other. The dildo was so thick and filled her up so well! The pleasure was hot and urgent within her, and she moaned Kevin's name, wishing he were there with her.

"Smack yourself," Kevin whispered. She obeyed, knowing what he wanted. Sometimes when Kevin played with her, drawing an orgasm from her with his fingers, he would alternately slap and then rub her pussy. She adored the sudden sharp contact of his hard fingers, which would dissolve into pure pleasure, intensified by the sting.

She pulled the now slick phallus from her dripping pussy and slapped her own sex with her free hand, the sound resounding in the quiet room. "Again," her master commanded her, and she obeyed.

Needing it too much, she pressed the rubber cock back into her pussy and began to fuck herself in earnest. Her moans and cries were no longer for his audience, but were wrenched from her lips as she rode higher and higher on the crest of her climax. "Oh God!" she screamed.

"Come for me," Kevin ordered, his breathing labored as he strained to keep quiet himself.

Kate rammed the hard cock inside of herself, her fingers dancing wildly over her clit, her body arched up from the rug. Still she kept the phone lodged at her ear; this was, after all, for her man. When finally her breathing slowed, she heard a distinct click. Someone had just rung off the line.

"Oh my god," she whispered, the pleasure draining suddenly away. "Kevin! What was that?"

Kevin laughed, and then said, "Must have been Nancy. She's always picking up my line instead of hers. She must have got an earful!" He seemed to think it was funny, but Kate had been horrified, and then chagrined. He teased her lightly, telling her not to worry. "She works for *me*, not the other way around! What I do on the phone is none of her business! She wouldn't dare say a word, don't worry. She's probably in the bathroom right now, those thick old support hose around her ankles, her hand buried in her crotch!"

Kate found the image at once repugnant and hilarious. She had laughed despite herself. Kevin then told her what a lovely, beautiful, sexy girl she was. Mollified, she let him go and returned to her vacuuming, humming happily as she worked.

She was a housewife, she supposed, though they weren't married and so far had never mentioned the possibility. She didn't miss her life out in the workaday world at all, though she knew this pampered life of hers might not last forever. She was happy now though, deeply content, and if she was considered a housewife, that suited her fine. She looked down at her bare breasts. The chains of gold dangling from her nipples reflected a butterscotch hint of sunlight through the large bay window. No, she thought to herself, smiling, more of a house-slave. Just the word whispering in her mind sent shivers of pleasure through the young woman. The party she'd attended with Amy had exceeded her wildest expectations. It wasn't the semi-naked slave girls and boys, or the Doms and Dommes dressed up in their requisite black leather, sporting whips and crops at their sides. That stuff was mostly for show, and she understood that it was a game for the majority of guests there that evening.

No, it had been the man standing by one of the many open bars, a fluted champagne glass in his hand, as he casually talked to a woman in a bustier and stiletto heels. At her feet was a slavish young man licking her red leather shoe while she completely ignored him.

When the man, who would later be introduced to her as Kevin, suddenly looked in her direction, it was as if something sparked through the air between them. It was just like in her corny romance novels! When their eyes met, suddenly Kate didn't hear the music from the live Brazilian band that was playing beside the well-lit swimming pool. She didn't hear the myriad of conversations going on all around them. She saw through the crowds of people milling in groups of twos and threes. She literally only had eyes for him.

It had only lasted a few seconds, when their eyes locked, but for Kate, her heart had been lost at that moment. Or found. Their connection had been immediate and the intensity had never lifted. When he approached her a few minutes later with a mutual acquaintance, it was somehow understood between them that they would be leaving the party together.

From that day on, they were inseparable. When he asked her to move in with him, she didn't hesitate for a second. And though they didn't discuss the future, the present was all Kate wanted, as long as it included Kevin.

From their first interaction, Kevin made it clear that he was the "master" and she was the "slave". But the connection was a loving one, full of romance and tenderness. It was understood that she "belonged" to him, in every sense, and this suited them both.

It wasn't a stifling relationship though, not at all. While Kevin was possessive, he never behaved jealously, or limited her friendships or time spent out of the house. She went where she liked, when she liked. She just found that what she liked most was being with him, or being there for him when he came home from a long day's work.

It was a romantic connection—no stern taskmaster whipping his charge until she bled. No sleeping in a cage in his closet, always in chains. Kevin had told Kate about some people he knew who lived this kind of harsh S&M

lifestyle, but it wasn't for him. No, what they had was more of a "service" kind of submission. Kate served her master, her lover, through sexual obedience and playful "torture" sessions. These games invariably ended in passionate lovemaking that left them both spent, happily asleep in each other's arms. Kate took deep, intense pleasure in serving her lord and master, in kneeling naked at the door, her head down, when he came home from work.

He would touch the top of her head, indicating she should stand, and she would gracefully unfold, lifting her pretty face sweetly for a kiss, her eyes closed in anticipated rapture. Sometimes he would press her shoulder instead, a signal that she should kneel completely down, her head touching the floor.

This always caused her poor pussy to become soaked, as she knew this promised a whipping. Kate loved the lash, had come to crave it. Kevin would take whatever implement Kate had chosen for the day and use it against her lovely creamy skin until she was moaning and writhing in the grip of the delicious combination of pleasure and erotic pain.

This gave her a special thrill—that *she* was charged with choosing the instrument of her loving torture. Each evening she was to wait naked and kneeling, save for those cuffs, which never left her wrists, with a whip, paddle or crop at her side. He may choose to use it or not, depending on his whim. The anticipation was almost as delicious as the actual delivery.

That night Kate was kneeling, her glossy auburn hair falling in pretty waves over bare shoulders, when the key scraped in the lock and Kevin entered, only his fine leather shoes were in her line of sight. She felt his hand on her head and she rose, awaiting her kiss.

He did kiss her, but perfunctorily, she thought with a tiny flash of irritation. Usually his kiss would consume her, lighting a fire in her belly that wouldn't be quenched until much later that night, after a fine dinner, brandy and finally sweet, hot lovemaking.

But Kevin had something to say, and he was too excited to hold back the news. "Kate! Mark is in town! Mark Lewis! He's coming to stay with us for the weekend, as soon as he's done with his meetings in town. Mark!" Kevin grinned, a slightly lopsided but wholly engaging smile that always melted Kate's heart.

And yet, his words caused a hint of anxiety, though she quickly dismissed it. Mark Lewis was Kevin's old college buddy. But more than that, he was his old lover. Kevin had shared, in some detail, his sexual adventures in college, about his homosexual explorations, and his love affair with the exciting and dangerous Mark.

Mark and Kevin were both bisexual, though Mark leaned more toward the gay end of the spectrum, and Kevin more toward the straight. Kevin had told Kate that while he liked to "play" with other men, it was only with a woman that he could make a lasting and meaningful emotional connection.

Kevin had hesitated to talk about it at first, but Kate had assured him she wouldn't judge him, or find him less desirable because of his past gay relationships. Indeed, she was fascinated, and eager to understand what would motivate a man like Kevin, a man who was dominant with women, to submit sexually to another man.

"Well, you know," he'd explained, "there's a thing called a 'switch'. Where you are dominant with some people, but submissive with others. Most people are like you, Kate, either one way or the other—submissive or dominant."

He laughed a little and commented, "Just like most people are either straight or gay, I guess, but in that case too, I go either way. Mostly my impulses are dominant, and always with women they are. That's just the way I'm hard-wired.

"But with some men, well, with one man in particular, I've always been submissive. I haven't actually been with that many guys, really. I mean, I was more active in my wild college days, which is when I met Mark. Even before our relationship became sexual, he was definitely the dominant force. He was the active one—I was more passive. He was the popular guy, I guess you could say, and I was his 'sidekick'. It worked for both of us, and when it turned sexual between us, it naturally extended to that aspect of our relationship."

He paused, looking in the distance, as if recalling that time. "For me it was just about fun. It was daring and exotic, both the gay play, and the D/s stuff. To tell you the truth, Mark was more into it than I was. More into me, if you will." Kevin smiled, looking a little embarrassed. He continued, "I mean, don't get me wrong, I always thought he was a great guy, but, as I explained to him, I could never connect that way with another man. It's just not part of my nature."

Stroking Kate's cheek tenderly, he said, "No, my nature is to be with a woman. That's where my heart lies. With you, Kate, my lovely and perfect woman."

Kate smiled, still intrigued with his bisexuality, but content to let the conversation die, as Kevin's fingers trailed down her neck, to her nipples and past her belly, to the sweet, hot center of her.

"Let's talk about Mark later," he'd murmured, as he kissed her neck, and Kate agreed that was a good idea.

She did bring it up again, though, as they were lying in bed, each with a good book propped against their knees. In theory, Kate had found the whole idea of Kevin's homosexual dalliances quite exciting. In theory, the thought of two strong, sexy men locked in a sensual but manly embrace was highly erotic to her. In theory. But now, faced with the very real prospect of meeting Kevin's onetime lover — his male lover, Kate felt confused, maybe even jealous.

Where would she fit in with this man?

"He's coming this Saturday. He'll stay the weekend. I want everything perfect. Of course, the finest sheets for the guest bed, and fresh flowers in every room. Why don't you make that delicious mushroom-stuffed trout thing you do? He'll love that! And maybe as an appetizer you could make that artichoke dip I love. And dessert, let's see," Kevin squinted up at the ceiling, as if the idea might be painted there. Apparently it was, as he said, "Yes, the raspberry chocolate torte thing, how about that?"

Kevin grinned at his slave girl, his face alight with excitement. Kate stifled her jealous impulse. She did love cooking for guests, and they hadn't had anyone over for a couple of weeks. It was a departure for Kevin to suggest the menu, but Mark was obviously a very special friend indeed.

Chapter Two

Saturday came and instead of sleeping late as he usually did on weekends, Kevin was up by six, and already working out in their exercise room when Kate peeked in. She had wrapped herself in the sheer silk robe he allowed her when she wasn't to be completely naked. The robe accentuated the nudity beneath it, rather than covering it, but it did add a modicum of warmth on this almost brisk September morning. Summer was nearing its end. Kate clutched the robe around herself and watched Kevin silently for a moment.

He had already worked up a sweat and his finely muscled chest and shoulders were straining under the weight of many pounds of steel. Kate admired his long lean torso, appreciating for the thousandth time his finely honed but not overbuilt muscles. Unlike some men, who focused exclusively on their upper bodies, Kevin had fine strong legs as well, with solid thighs and shapely calves.

Kate licked her lips as she watched her lover, quashing the feeling of unease. Instead of sleeping, he was "buffing up" for Mark. He looked over at Kate and a smile broke on his face. "Hey, lazybones! Decided to get your sweet ass out of bed at last, eh? I'm almost done here. Wait a second and you can join me in the shower. Drop your robe. Let me see perfection while I finish here."

Smiling shyly, Kate dropped her robe. Her tall lean form, with her narrow hips and shapely legs was saved from girlishness by her full lush breasts. She felt her nipples tighten against the golden rods that had pierced her flesh just last month.

Kate had been frightened, truly frightened. Needles terrified her. And yet, in spite of that fear, or perhaps partially because of it, she was deeply intrigued by the idea of Kevin piercing her flesh and slipping the pretty gold jewelry he'd shown her through her nipples.

At first she'd said, "No." It was that simple. He'd brought up the idea of piercing her, and she'd said no, out of hand. "I hate needles," she explained. "Just the thought of them makes me sick! I will never, ever let you do that to me, so just forget it. Forget it! End of story!" He had smiled, raising his eyebrows slightly. He didn't bring up her promise to obey him in all things, and her supposed desire to suffer for him. He understood that this fell outside the realm of their sexual games. If Kate said no, that was that.

But the idea had played in her mind for days. Kevin didn't say another word, and yet the possibility continued to whisper, taking hold in Kate's mind. She even went online, looking to learn more about it.

The testimonials she read on various piercing sites ran the gamut from, "The worst pain I ever experienced," to "Just a slight pinch". She didn't know what to think. She looked at the little kits you could order to do the piercing at home. Kevin had said he'd like to be the one to do it. He'd done it before, he told her, twice, though never for a lover. He had done it for friends in the scene, because he wasn't squeamish about needles at all, and had a steady hand. If it were going to be done at all—which it wasn't, she told herself—she would rather Kevin do it, than have it done in some seedy piercing parlor, exposing herself in some refurbished dentist chair, mauled by a mohawked youth with a pierced tongue and a multitude of tattoos.

Kevin didn't bring it up again. He had said she might come to change her mind, and to feel free to research it, or ask him anything about it. It wasn't that important, he'd assured her, kissing her on the forehead.

Kate didn't pursue the matter, but it bothered her. It was the first and only time she'd said, "no" to him. She had promised herself she would always try to obey him, as it thrilled and delighted her submissive nature to do so, and also pleased him enormously. They were, as they were both fond of saying, a perfect fit. Now it seemed a new groove had been cut by her refusal that left them ever so slightly "out of alignment".

Still, she appreciated that he didn't press her, or harp on it. Before she had become so seriously involved with a dominant man, she'd had vague ideas about Doms forcing their subs to submit to all sorts of terrible and degrading, even dangerous things. She had, as many do, confused submission with abuse.

Kevin was nothing like that, and indeed, went to great lengths to assure her that anyone who did behave that way was little more than a bully. "The beauty of it, what gives submission its power, is that it's consensual. It's something offered, not necessarily easily, but freely. That is the essence of a loving D/s relationship. At least in my book!" Then he'd laughed, looking slightly embarrassed. Kevin tended to get on a soapbox when it came to consensual submission. He hated the posturing he so often saw at play parties, with silly men "demanding" that their "worthless" slaves submit to some play torture or other. It might be all right as a game, but Kevin said he found it insulting.

Regarding the nipple rings, Kevin had been clever. He'd done with Kate what many a Dom had done before him, which was to introduce an idea his sub first dismissed out of hand and then was left to ponder. Though she didn't mention it, he was aware that she had gone online to check out the piercing sites. He saw her a few times, when she thought she was unobserved, touching her nipple, pinching it, as she stared into space.

One thing he did do was place a little jewelry box on the dining room table one morning, just before he left for work.

Kate came out of the kitchen where she had been washing up, to kiss him goodbye, a last lingering kiss. He took the small velvet box out his briefcase, just as he was almost out the door. "Oh," he said, feigning innocence, "I almost forgot. I got this the other day. Just in case we might want it sometime." He set the little box on the table, next to one of Kate's pretty flower arrangements, this time sunflowers and marigolds. After he'd gone, Kate went over to the box and opened it, as clearly he'd meant for her to do.

Inside was a pair of little gold bars, barely thicker than a paperclip, if it were opened up. They were of a very fine gold, with a slight pinkish hue. Each end was capped with a little diamond, set in a screw-on ball, so that they could be removed. Dangling from each little bar was a delicate gold chain with a tiny diamond heart set at the center. As Kate held up the nipple jewelry, for that is what it was, the little diamonds caught and reflected the morning light coming in through the east window.

Kate was entranced. She'd seen pictures of nipple jewelry, but it had just been the standard barbells, of silver or steel, or little hoops or horseshoes. This was clearly fine jewelry, precious jewelry. She could tell the gold was quality, probably twenty-four karat, and the diamonds, while small, were real and finely cut, glittering in her hand.

She took the jewelry to the bathroom and stood naked in front of the mirror, turning this way and that, holding the bars against her nipples as if they had already been inserted. Carefully she unscrewed one of the little diamond clasps, imagining that thin rod of gold inserted through her nipple. Well, at least with these screw-on clasps, it wasn't permanent. She could remove the jewelry whenever she wanted. This gave Kate comfort, and then it startled her, because she realized she was already thinking in a way that meant she had decided to do it.

She was glad he had picked gold; it went with her coppery auburn hair and her dark brown eyes, and of course, diamonds were never out of place! "You are insane," she said aloud to herself in the mirror. Taking the jewelry with her, and placing it carefully back in its velvet nest, she left it on the dining room table and went to the computer in search of more information.

That night the box still sat where Kevin had left it. If he noticed, he made no remark. Nor did Kate. She served him a lovely dinner, as always, and the little box sat silently near the flowers, ostensibly ignored.

But later that night, when Kevin was on top of her, his cock pressed deep inside of her, his hands holding hers high above her head on the bed, Kate whispered, "I think I want it."

Kevin didn't reply at first. She wasn't even sure if he'd heard, so taken was he with her soft yielding body responding beneath his. He moved in her slowly, drawing them both to a sweet surrender, but he paused after a bit and whispered back, "You want what?"

"The jewelry. I want you to do it. You know."

"Say it."

"Oh, Kevin."

"If you can't even say it, then surely you aren't ready. Give it time, love. We have all the time in the world." He took her then, no longer slowly and sweetly, but roughly, biting her neck as he held her down, fucking her until she screamed in ecstasy, sending them both over the edge.

It was Kate who procured the kit. She found one online that looked safe and easy to use. It wasn't the cheapest, but nor was it the most expensive. It simply looked to be the best, and testimonials from users promised excellent and safe results. One night about a week after she'd hinted that she'd like the piercing, she presented the kit to Kevin.

As always, she was kneeling naked near the front door, eager for his return. But this time, instead of a whip or crop nearby, there sat a little package containing needles, corks, clamps and other items apparently necessary, all wrapped securely in clear plastic. It was a moment before Kevin noticed it, but when he picked it up, he knew right away what it was. Still, he teased Kate a bit, drawing a blush from her, as he demanded, "Ah, and what have we here? How in the world did this get here? I know my slave girl wouldn't have ordered it! She's terrified of needles. There's no way my Kate would ever allow her nipples to be pierced. End of story."

Kate laughed, embarrassed, and playfully punched Kevin's arm. "Stop it, you bastard! Don't make me crazy! I want it. I've done the research, like you said. I think they're beautiful. And I love the symbolism of it, that you would pierce me, mark me permanently, and adorn me with gems and gold just like some ancient harem slave, adored by the king. You are my king." She whispered the last words, wrapping her arms around him, her body naked against his fine suit jacket.

That night Kevin bound Kate against the wall in their playroom. He had paneled a portion of the wall with padded fabric for extended play sessions. Kate was secured against that wall, which had stout hooks placed strategically on it. She was tethered by a leather collar around her throat, as well as by her wrists and ankles.

She wasn't bound in order to keep her still, but because it aroused her so to be chained this way, shackled to the wall like a prisoner in a dungeon. Of course, unlike a real dungeon, instead of being cruelly beaten and starved, here she was teased and adored, and the "torture" was a delicious pleasure to her.

Because of her still very real fear of needles, Kevin blindfolded her with a long piece of red silk he kept for that purpose. She had asked if she might lie down, but Kevin explained that he wanted the jewelry to rest naturally against her, and her breast position would change if she lay down.

She understood, and so now stood, tethered against the soft wall, helpless before her master. Her legs were spread wide, and Kevin's fingers were playing against her silky bare sex, drawing moisture from her, making her swell and moan with need. Her nipples were distended and swollen as well. This would make her more sensitive to the sharp prick of the needle, but that sensitivity would hopefully be offset by her arousal.

She actually wanted it now. Didn't just want to submit to his will, or to have the results of the pretty jewelry. She wanted the piercing. She wanted to submit to Kevin, to feel the prick followed by the jewelry as it slipped into place, marking her in a new, beautiful way, as belonging to him.

"Here," Kevin said, touching a glass of brandy to Kate's lips. She took a drink of it, and another. It burned sweetly in her chest.

"Are you ready, darling?" Kevin asked, holding the needle near her breast. Kate, blindfolded, nodded, licking her lips and took a deep breath.

"That's right," Kevin said, "deep and slow. Just breathe deep and slow. I'll tell you when I'm going to do it, but you just keep breathing deep and slow. It's very quick."

And it had been. It had hurt, no mistake about it. And the second one had hurt more than the first, probably because she was now anticipating its bite. She might have fainted, falling to the floor, if it hadn't been for the leather binding her at the neck, wrists and ankles. But she had withstood it, and felt a wonderful pride rushing through her veins when Kevin announced that he was done.

Instead of releasing her right away, Kevin made love to her perfect body for some minutes, kissing her skin all over, savoring the sweetness of her, pausing a long time at her spread cleft. He didn't stop until she was earnestly begging to be allowed to come. He let her, holding her against the wall as she shuddered and jerked in her chains.

Only then did he let her down, quickly releasing the clasps that held her and taking her gently in his arms. He led her to the bathroom, where they both marveled at how beautifully the gold glinted against her breasts. The nipples were dark red, as if blushing at what had been done to them. Kate was delighted. She understood on an intimate level now what was meant when they said "true submissives" were brave. She felt as brave as a knight! And because she'd stood up to her own fears, she felt empowered.

Kate's nipples were very tender for about a week. She couldn't even bear Kevin's lightest touch against her. But they quickly healed, aided by a soothing balm that had come with the kit. Now she loved the nipple rings; they made her feel feminine and vulnerable. Many times a day she paused in her work to examine her beautiful nipple jewelry. She especially loved the way the little delicate gold chains hung down below each nipple, gently swaying against her breasts as she moved. The little diamond hearts caught the light, reflecting and refracting it against their many facets.

Kevin adored the rings as well. He wanted her to sit bare at the table, closer than she usually did, so he could finger and fondle the jewelry, teasing her nipples to arousal with just a touch. Along with just being a sexy new thing they had done together, the piercing itself had deepened their relationship. Kate had truly submitted to Kevin, doing something that frightened her, because he asked it of her.

Now when they made love, Kevin would bite and tease her nipples, pulling gently on the chains with his teeth. The little bars resting snugly through Kate's nipples would twist and turn as he did this. Kate trusted Kevin completely, and yet the little thrill of danger, danger that he might pull too hard, actually heightened the experience of lovemaking.

Now, dropping his weights, standing tall in just his shorts, Kevin gazed at his lover appreciatively, his eye following the line of her smooth, hard belly, down to her mons, shaved bare. "Show me your pussy, slave," he said, his voice stern but his eyes dancing. Flushing, even though he commanded this several times a day and she should have been used to it, Kate obediently spread her legs, arching up slightly so he could see the sweet pussy lips peeking out from between her legs. Could he see the moistness his request had caused?

Kevin came over to her, wiping sweat from his brow with a thick white towel. Together they went to the large master bathroom, where Kate started the shower running. Kevin had had his shower specially designed. It not only contained the traditional showerhead, but also had spigots on three sides of the stall, which was quite large enough to easily accommodate two.

They stepped in together, Kate kneeling as she was accustomed to do, ready to suck her lover's cock until it was rock-hard. Then she was to soap him up, wash and rinse his hair and body, suck his cock until he exploded in her mouth, and then, and only then, wash herself.

To her surprise, Kevin pulled her up by an arm. "Not today, sweetheart. Today I have to save myself for Mark! You have to save yourself too. No sex, or at least no orgasms, until tonight, in his presence."

Save himself for Mark! The lurking unease and jealousy now burst forth in full flower as Kate retorted, "Save yourself for Mark! Jesus, Kevin, I thought he was a passing affair from fifteen years ago, not your fucking lover!" She immediately bit her lip and looked away. She had never, in the three months they'd been together, raised her voice to him, or protested any of his actions, sexual or otherwise.

Kevin looked at her, abashed. He was startled by the vehemence of her outburst and surprised by her decidedly un-submissive behavior. But then he slowly smiled and took Kate gently in his arms. "Katie, baby. Katie-cat. I do believe you're jealous."

She started to protest, to apologize, but he cut her off, pressing her close to his chest, letting the hot water spray over them both. "Sweetheart, please, please don't be jealous! Yes, I am excited, nervous even, about Mark coming. You see, I haven't told you everything." Kate tensed; here it came. He was going to leave her for this Mark person.

Kevin went on, unaware of the depth of her insecurity, "Yeah, Mark and I met in college, but we've always stayed friends, and have seen each other maybe a dozen times since then, whenever he passes through town. I told you how Mark and I fooled around, right? But I didn't tell you all the details. You know how you're my lovely submissive slave girl? Well, I was his. His boy toy. His sub."

Kate laughed, despite her misgivings. Though he'd told her before he was submissive with men, this idea didn't fit in with her notion of Kevin as a strong dominant man. Sensing her disbelief Kevin explained, "It was a game, of course. Nothing like what we have. At first, I was just beginning to explore my interest and developing passion for the D/s lifestyle and BDSM games. We both were. He was naturally dominant, and when he exerted his will over me, it was easy to comply, to give in, to obey. It was thrilling, really, as I know it must be for you. That total loss of control. The trust it requires to give yourself over, sexually and completely, to another person. The submersion of self in the ecstasy of submission."

Kate smiled. She understood perfectly, and said, "Kevin. I had no idea you had submissive impulses. And yet, with me you're so dominant. So assured and in control."

"And with you, my love, I wouldn't have it any other way. I adore you, and I cherish your sweet and giving nature, your willingness to obey me in all things. So obey me now, little one. And trust that I love you, and whatever we might have or do with Mark this weekend will only be a testament of our love for each other. An extension, if you will. And when you serve him, and serve him you shall, you will also be serving me."

Chapter Three

Kate checked her face and figure for the fifth time in the bedroom mirror. She was dressed simply, in a silky shift of shimmering green with nothing underneath. Her heavy but still high breasts were hidden under silk that hung down in soft folds, revealing her sexy cleavage, but hiding the ever-present gold and diamonds at her breasts. Below the breasts, the dress fit smoothly against her lithe form, accenting her slightly flaring hips, ending just at the knee. The rich emerald green of the dress complemented her coppery auburn hair, which was pulled back in a loose French braid trailing down her back.

Thoughts raced through her head, though she hadn't voiced them to Kevin. How would she feel, watching her man submit to another man? Not just playing around, maybe kissing and whatever, but actually submitting sexually to him, as she did with Kevin? Would this man whip her lover? Would Kevin be forced to his knees, forced to take another man's cock down his throat?

Kate had to admit that the idea was at once frightening and exciting. She had only known Kevin as the one in complete control. He was her "lord and master" by design and desire. Would she still be able to respect and obey a man who let another man use him as he used her?

And where would it leave her? Would this Mark be at all interested in a woman? Or was his sole focus to be with his "boy toy", while Kate was relegated to the sidelines, jealously watching two lovers who hadn't time for a mere "girl"?

Hush, she told herself, still your mind. Kevin had taught her relaxation techniques as a part of "grace" training. Now she consciously stilled her mind, letting the thoughts rise and glide away. She loved and trusted Kevin. Whatever happened this weekend was what Kevin wanted. If she was afraid he would run off with his gay lover, then the two of them, she and Kevin, had far less than she believed. If that were the case, better to find out now. Kate willed her thoughts to quiet even from these reflections. She felt her mind empty, her pulse slow, her breathing deepen.

Slowly she opened her eyes, looking at the young woman who now smiled back at her in the mirror. She was barefoot, but added her wrist cuffs. She also wore ankle cuffs and a matching leather slave collar around her delicate throat. From the center of the collar hung an oblong gold hoop, which could be used to easily tether her where her master wished. The wrist and ankle cuffs had similar hoops, and had been much used in their bondage games.

Her large dark eyes crinkled a little at the corners as she grinned at herself. "Lighten up!" she admonished herself aloud. "This is going to fun!"

The food was ready, and the table lavishly set with Kevin's finest linen tablecloth and napkins, real silverware and cut crystal, and one of Kate's artfully arranged vases of fresh flowers as a beautiful centerpiece. Kevin was sitting in the living room, ostensibly reading his magazine, but if one observed him closely, he never turned a page. Instead he was staring out the large window into their backyard, his eyes resting on the sunken swimming pool, its water sparkling now, dappled with light from the setting sun.

The doorbell rang and Kevin dropped his magazine at the same time as Kate emerged from the bedroom. "Shall I get it?" she asked.

"We'll go together," Kevin said, another departure, as Kate always got the door and answered the telephone. When he opened the door, Kate stood slightly back, smiling uncertainly.

In stepped the man who must be Mark. Kate was surprised, as he couldn't be taller than five foot, eight inches, compared with Kevin's six foot, two! Somehow, she had imagined that someone who had dommed her lover would be big and strong. Without realizing it, she'd imagined Mark to be a big burly bear of a man. Instead, this fellow could almost be described as dapper.

Compared to Kevin's open Irish good looks, with his bright blue eyes and shock of strawberry blond hair, Mark was darker, with closely cropped brown hair, the hairline receding against a high well-shaped forehead and deep-set, dark eyes.

There was a sort of coiled strength in him though, that belied the small lean frame. One got the sense somehow that this wasn't a man to trifle with. Right now, his face was creased into a huge smile, as he and Kevin leaned forward in a tight embrace.

He dropped a large sort of briefcase he was carrying and Kevin laughed, "Never travel without your bag of tricks, eh? Got anything new and evil?"

"But of course," Mark laughed back. "I would never come to you empty-handed!" Mark stood back a moment, appraising his friend. "It's been too long, too long. How have you been, my little boy toy?"

Kevin glanced at Kate, coloring a little at Mark's use of his old submissive nickname. Perhaps to regain an upper hand he now said, "Allow me to present my submissive, Kate. Please consider her yours for the evening. Kate?"

His question to her was an unspoken but rehearsed one. She was to drop into a curtsey when introduced. She noted as she knelt, prettily holding the edges of her silken dress, that he had "presented" her to Mark, as opposed to introducing the man first to the woman, as was traditional in polite society.

Mark looked at her now, and said, "Kate. Are you Kevin's sub? Are you owned by him?"

Kate felt the heat creeping up her face in a hot flush. She looked down at the floor, still crouched in a curtsey, and nodded. Was she owned by him? She had never put it in precisely those terms, but something about the phrase sent an electric jolt of excitement through her loins.

"Stand up," Mark commanded, and she did, rising to a height that equaled his own. Mark stepped very close and said softly, "It's a pleasure to meet you, slave. I think we're going to have a wonderful time this weekend."

Kevin cleared his throat a little, and taking Mark's arm said, "Let me show you around. Kate will bring us a little refreshment." To Kate: "You can serve us out back, Kate." As the two men walked into the living room, Kate stood still a moment, nonplussed. She felt as if she had just been dismissed as a maid or servant might be. Serve us out back, indeed! She felt the excitement fading, replaced again by the unease she had felt earlier.

Still, she would be the gracious hostess, and serve the men out by the pool. She picked up the tray of little snacks prepared beforehand, and brought it out back, setting out the items for easy access between two pool chairs. The sun had slipped below the horizon, coloring the pool a rich azure that matched the darkening sky. Even barefoot Kate was still comfortable, as it had been a sunny day, and the granite that surrounded the pool area still retained the heat.

In a few moments, the men came out. Both were dressed casually in jeans and open-necked shirts. They held bottles of beer, and Kevin offered Kate one, which she accepted with thanks, cradling the cold glass between her palms.

Once the two men were seated, Kate knelt at Kevin's feet, leaning back against his legs. His hand idly smoothed her forehead, and then dropped down to her breast. Kate glanced at Mark, a little embarrassed that Kevin was fondling her in front of him, but he didn't seem to notice, or if he did, he made no remark.

They caught up on old times for a while. Both men were in business, and they engaged in the typical male banter about their latest successful deal. They exchanged a few stories about old classmates they still knew, and tidbits about their families. Kate listened, interested in seeing this different side of Kevin, who rarely talked with her about the past. She wasn't invited to participate, and being a natural listener, she didn't mind.

If Mark was even aware of Kate kneeling at her lover's feet, he gave no sign. His focus was entirely on Kevin, even when remarking that the dip was delicious. His compliments went not to the chef, but to her "owner".

So she was surprised, not expecting to be addressed when suddenly Mark said, "Kate, stand up." She looked to Kevin, who nodded slightly. He had told her over and over during the preceding week that when Mark arrived, he called all the shots, period. Whatever Mark said was the law, for both of them, for this one weekend. Kate had agreed, though she wasn't certain to what she was agreeing. She was about to find out.

She stood, unconsciously sucking in her belly and thrusting her breasts slightly forward. Mark asked, "Is this backyard secure? Can anyone see us?"

"Completely secure," Kevin answered, as he waved toward the twelve-foot fences that surrounded the spacious lawn and pool area. "And behind those fences is another acre of undeveloped land. We could dance naked back here if we wanted and no one would ever be the wiser."

"That's what I was hoping you'd say," Mark grinned, his eyes now raking Kate's long sexy body clad in silk. "Let's lose that dress, shall we, slave girl?"

Lose the dress? For a split second, Kate actually didn't know what he meant. As realization dawned, she stood rooted to the spot, staring dumbly back at him.

"Not terribly obedient, is she, Kevin? Or is she just slow? Stupid? *Problema con Ingles?*"

Kevin looked embarrassed, his features darkening. Mark's first command and Kate was standing there like a statue. More harshly than perhaps he'd intended, Kevin barked. "Go on, Kate. You heard the man. Strip!"

Kate's eyes teared at his unkind tone, but she obeyed, slowly lifting the edges of her dress, pulling it free over her head. She dropped the garment on the warm granite and stood still before the appraising eyes of the two men.

She looked to Kevin for approval, and saw that he was looking not at her, but at Mark. Mark, on the other hand, was burning a hole through her with his eyes. They were dark, even smoldering, as he looked slowly up and down her lithe and slender form. She looked down, trying to still her mind, her heart. This was for Kevin. This was for Kevin. The words echoed silently like a little mantra and she calmed herself.

"She's lovely," Mark said, though it almost sounded perfunctory. "But you know, I like a woman to be shaved. Easier to whip her cunt." He touched her bare mons with two fingers and Kate stayed perfectly still, realizing that she was holding her breath. How odd to have this strange man touching her in this intimate way, while her lover sat by, his expression bemused. Yet, she found herself becoming very aroused, as if she were a slave girl on the auction block in one of her historical romances. Mark dropped his hand and stood back.

"And these!" Mark whistled a long low whistle, reaching out to Kate's pierced nipples. "Aren't those unusual?" Turning to Kevin he asked, "May I?" gesturing toward Kate's round pretty breasts. He hadn't asked Kate, of course. She was simply the sub. Again, that confusion surged through her, at once affronted and yet deeply aroused by being treated as a sex object. Her opinion or desire didn't enter into it. This was between the men.

Kevin smiled that slow big smile of his, pride sparkling in his eyes. It clearly mattered a great deal to him what Mark thought. He nodded, waving his hand at Kate, saying, "By all means, look and touch all you like. As

I said earlier, Kate is yours for the weekend. You don't need to ask permission."

Mark nodded, as gracious as a king, and stood directly in front of Kate. He cupped each breast in a hand, lifting them gently and letting them fall. The little chains swayed erotically, the diamonds glinting in the lowering sun. "Beautiful," Mark murmured, and Kate blushed. Something about this man frightened her. There was something hard, even dangerous, in his bearing. And yet, that was silly! He was an old and dear friend of Kevin's. Kevin would never put her in danger. She tried to smile at Mark, who grinned back a wolfish grin, dropping her breasts and stepping back.

Kevin smiled, unaware of any tension between his two lovers. He stepped toward Kate, taking her protectively in his arms. "She is my greatest treasure," he said, kissing the top of her head. "You're wonderful," he whispered in her ear. "You're my angel."

Feeling somewhat reassured, Kate smiled up at him, and kissed him back when he kissed her mouth. "Take down her hair," Mark ordered. Kevin removed the few pins that held Kate's braid in place. She shook her head, releasing the coppery waves of thick hair. Both men looked at her, the lust obvious in both their faces, and the pride in Kevin's. She smiled happily up at her master.

"Whatever's in that oven smells fantastic," Mark commented, sniffing toward the open backdoor, a clear cue that he was hungry. Kate knelt down to retrieve her dress but Mark stopped her, his hand on her wrist. His grip was firm, his fingers strong.

"No," he said. "I want you naked. You'll be naked for the rest of the weekend. That's how I like my subs. Those leather cuffs are all you'll be needing, slave."

Kate resisted her impulse to look to Kevin for approval. She sensed somehow that this would embarrass him, cause a loss of face. She was to obey Mark without question. She didn't require Kevin's prior permission to obey Mark. And the fact that Mark was directing Kevin's slave — ordering her to strip for him, and dictating that she stay that way — was another way in which Mark was also laying claim to Kevin. What was Kevin's was now Mark's, and Mark's word would supersede Kevin's, at least for tonight.

The fish was perfect, nicely balanced with fresh asparagus and home-baked corn muffins. Kate sat naked with the clothed men but actually found it didn't trouble her much; she was used to being naked around Kevin, and she knew her body appealed to men, apparently even gay men.

When no one could eat another bite, Mark leaned over and tugged gently at Kate's nipple chain. "These really are beautiful, Kevin. Who did the piercing for you?"

"I did it myself," Kevin said, smiling. "Kate was very brave."

"Did it hurt, Kate?" Mark asked, his eyes curiously bright.

"Like a mother-fucker!" Kate said emphatically. They all laughed as the tension visibly eased in the room.

Too full to appreciate dessert, the three adjourned to the living room, where Kate served Grand Marnier brandy in large snifters. She settled again at Kevin's feet.

As they sipped the fine orange brandy, Kate leaned into Kevin's legs, relaxing her bare back against him. She felt happy and confident that the meal had gone well. They had continued their "small talk" over dinner, as if it were perfectly natural that the hostess should be naked and pierced as she served the vegetables, or leaned over a glass to pour more wine.

She felt the shift of mood in the room, as if the "formalities" were now over and they could now get down to "business". They were silent as Kevin watched Mark, who was sipping his brandy and regarding Kevin and Kate through narrowed eyes. Again, Kate was struck with his power. It emanated from him like light, only denser.

Mark, leaning back in his chair said, "Kevin. Let me see you. Stand up, why don't you? It's been too long. Are you keeping in shape?"

Kevin pushed gently at Kate so he could rise, and stood in front of his old lover, as if for inspection. "Take off your shirt," Mark said, his voice pleasant, but the command clear.

Kevin unbuttoned his shirt and let it drop. His finely muscled chest gleamed in the soft light of the room, dark little blond curls traced down his sternum. Kate felt a swelling of pride at her lover's fine physique. But something else was at work as well. It was quite odd to have another person, a man, ordering Kevin to pose for him.

"Very nice, very nice," Mark said, actually licking his lips. "The jeans, if you please." Without the slightest blush or trace of embarrassment, Kevin dropped his pants. He was wearing silk bikini underwear that hugged his sizable endowment, which seemed to be growing by the second.

"Oh, yes," Mark grinned. "Kate, you are a lucky girl." Turning to Kevin he said, "Does she give good head?"

"Not bad," Kevin smiled, patting her head proprietarily.

Not bad! Kate prided herself on her ability to drive Kevin absolutely wild with her mouth. He had taught her to service him with her hands cuffed behind her back. She could lick and tease him to a frenzy, taking it as slow as she could, until he would lose control and grab her head, fucking her face until he shot his load deep into her throat.

"Can she do the breath test?"

"Oh," Kevin pursed his lips a moment, as if trying to recall what Mark meant. But he well knew. Hedging, he said, "Uh, not really. That is, we haven't really gone there yet."

"Well, we'll need to go there tonight, dear boy. You know how I like that."

The breath test? What was that? Kate knew instinctively she wasn't to be part of this conversation. She was to be seen and not heard. But she was curious. And a little anxious, as Kevin had seemed perturbed, even embarrassed, not to have taught her the "breath test", whatever that was!

Mark looked skeptically at Kate. "Well, let's test her mettle a bit then. Slave!" Mark turned his attention to the naked woman crouching on the floor. "Kneel up and put your hands behind you." Kate obediently assumed the position, one Kevin had taught her, sitting up so her torso was straight, breasts thrust out, knees spread wide so the view of her bare pussy was not hindered by her thighs.

She felt her heart thumping; it was beginning in earnest now. Mark came over to the two of them. First, he cuffed Kate's wrists behind her with the little clips that dangled there for that purpose. Moving to Kevin, he stood very close in front of the taller man and, slipping his fingers under the elastic on either hip, he pulled down the underwear, setting Kevin's sizable erection free. Pressing up against him, so that Kevin's penis was mashed between them, Mark pulled Kevin's head down with both hands and kissed him on the mouth. A lover's kiss, long and lingering.

Kevin responded as Kate watched, kneeling at their feet. She licked her own lips, trying to process the confusion of feelings—jealousy like a hot burn in her chest, but also something else. Arousal centered deep in her belly, making her pussy lips slippery with lust. The two men were hot, whether one of them was her lover or not. Had she been free to stand and do as she wished, she would have stood behind Kevin, sandwiching him between herself and Mark, rubbing herself against his strong back and tight sexy ass.

But she was not free. She was reminded of this when the two men broke away, or rather Mark did, pulling back from Kevin, who seemed to lean slightly toward him, as if he didn't want the kiss to stop.

Let's see what you can do, slut," Mark said to Kate. "Suck his gorgeous cock. Do it like you mean it. Impress me."

Kate scooted forward, eager to take her master's cock into her mouth, eager too to show Mark that she was no second-rate submissive, as he seemed to imply. Slowly she licked the head of Kevin's cock, savoring his sweet taste. She looked up at him, her eyes wide and full of love, and Kevin smiled down at her, his expression encouraging. Clearly, he wanted to impress Mark as well. She looked back down, focusing on his member, licking slowly down and then swirling up in butterfly circles, making him shudder with pleasure.

She felt his hands on her shoulders as he steadied himself. Opening her throat as he had taught her, she took his penis back and back, sliding her head down until she completely enveloped the shaft. Slowly she released it, bit by bit, wresting a moan from her lover.

Mark watched, his eyes again narrowed, sitting forward on the couch. Kate was aware of his eyes on them. It was exciting to have an observer. She knew she looked sexy, kneeling up, legs spread, hands bound behind her, a man's cock down her throat. She moved in and away, consciously sensual, striving to impress Kevin's strange lover.

After a few moments, Mark stood and went to the front hall where he'd left his bag of toys. Returning to find Kate still sucking and kissing her lover's cock, he addressed himself to Kevin. "Boy toy, let's add some fun to the, uh, proceedings. Does your sub take a good whipping?" As Kevin nodded, Mark said, "How about while she's sucking you off? Can she focus?"

Kate had never been whipped while sucking his penis. It was a curious proposition, but it seemed to appeal to Kevin, because he smiled slowly and said, "I really don't know, Mark. We haven't had that particular opportunity. Let's give it a try, shall we?"

"We shall, and I wasn't asking your permission," Mark said, making Kevin look quickly down, perhaps to cover his embarrassment at having overstepped with his dominant lover. Kevin now pulled Kate's head suddenly, thrusting his cock into her throat, making her gag and splutter, as she hadn't been ready.

Mark made a disapproving clucking sound as he moved behind the young woman, crouching low, a single lash in his hand. "Not very open to you, is she? I'd soon train that nonsense out of her." Kate bridled, but of course didn't openly respond to his taunt. She silently thanked the powers that be that she wasn't "his" and wouldn't be subjected to his "training". Slowly she tickled the underside of Kevin's cock with her tongue, drawing a sweet moan from him that made her smile.

Mark was close behind her; she could hear him breathing as he bent toward her, a whip in his hand. Unlike the heavy flogger that Kate favored, the single lash could mark and welt the flesh quickly, though it did no permanent damage. It packed a fiery sting, leaving long white lines that faded to dark pink.

Kate couldn't see Mark behind her. She knew she was going to be whipped, and hoped she could take it without smashing into Kevin, or inadvertently biting him! But she was unprepared for that nasty single lash when the first one caught her across both cheeks.

Kate gasped, the sound muffled by Kevin's cock filling her mouth. She lurched uncontrollably against Kevin, who caught and steadied her. "We don't usually use the single lash," he explained to Mark. We *never* use the single lash, corrected Kate silently, as the burn of it worked its way across her nerve endings.

Another line of fire spread across her butt cheeks, a little higher than the first. Kate was ready this time, but it still hurt! She did love a good whipping, but this was more like a cut than a sensual lashing. Kate began to breathe heavily, unable to control the edge of fear that pulsated against her consciousness. *Kevin!* she silently cried. Kevin, *he's hurting me!*

Again, the cruel bite of the single lash. Kevin must have felt her panic, but he only held her head, forcing his cock deep into her throat. As Mark continued to lash the bound girl, a curious and lovely, though not unfamiliar, change began to take place. It was something she loved, and sought, but it was rare in coming. You couldn't force the wonderfully intense submissive headspace that a skilled Dom could send a sub to. Even if you longed for its passion and possession, you couldn't will it. And for Kate, she had found that she had to "go through it" to get to it. She had to descend into a kind of purgatory of fear and pain, before she could arise out of it, triumphant and powerful in her submission.

It was so hard to explain to someone who had never experienced it. She and Kevin had talked about it. He thought he understood, though he himself had never "been there" as he said. He'd heard about it from other subs, not just Kate, and was perhaps a little jealous at the obvious intensity of experience she seemed to have. Language failed, and she let it go.

But now, as the center of attention in what felt dangerous but also wildly erotic, Kate felt that peculiar sensual lethargy settle over her, catching her securely in its net. She still felt the sting of Mark's whip, but it was overlain with a fierce, sweet pleasure. She longed to touch her own pussy, to soothe the heat being created by her curious circumstance, bound, her mouth stuffed with her lover's cock, another man whipping her bare ass from behind.

Mark continued to whip her, and she continued to kiss Kevin. Though almost in a trance, Kate was aware that her lover was about to come. She felt that sweet tensing of his body, and the shiver in his cock that signaled impending release.

Mark stood back, watching the pair a moment and then said, "Stop, girl. He isn't allowed. Not yet." Kate continued to suckle her lover; who was this man to tell her to stop? But Kevin pushed her head away, his face flushed, his breath coming in rapid little bursts. He would obey Mark and his expression reminded her that she was to obey as well.

Mark smiled evilly. "She's good, Kevin. She can take it. But she's no pro when it comes to giving you head, is she?" The sensual trance fell away, and Kate fought off her own rising anger. Who was this bastard, anyway? How could he sit there, watching her do what she knew she did so well, and say she was "no pro"? Even while being whipped with that lash, she had kept Kevin's shaft in her mouth, teasing and suckling him despite whatever Mark might do to her. What did he expect her to do, make Kevin's head explode?

She felt Mark's hand on her shoulder, pulling her back. Her bottom smarted from the sting, and any trace of sexual bliss had scattered like a dispelled fog.

"We'll have to show her how it's done, won't we, boy toy?"

Kevin gulped, his Adam's apple bobbing. He looked almost shy and Kate found suddenly that she wanted to hug him, to protect him from this man who was domming her master in front of her. "Come on, Kevin, show her how the pros do it. It takes another man to really suck cock properly, that's what I've always said."

Mark dropped his own jeans, stepping easily out of them. His legs were strong—the legs of an athlete. He pulled down his own underwear, also bikini briefs, and out popped a very thick penis with a bulbous head. Kevin's cock was larger and longer overall, Kate noted, but not as thick. She found herself wondering how it would feel to have that huge cockhead penetrate her. Flushing, she turned away.

Kevin knelt in front of Mark, his own cock still glistening from Kate's kisses. Kate, her hands still bound behind her, was left to fend for herself. She scooted closer to the two men, at once repelled and excited by the idea of Kevin taking a man's cock into his mouth.

Mark leaned down, grabbing a handful of Kevin's thick, curly hair. Pulling Kevin's head back, so that his mouth was offered up to him, Mark kissed him, long and passionately, while Kate fidgeted, wishing again she could touch her pussy.

Mark let Kevin go and positioned himself so that his erect cock bobbed in front of Kevin's face. He stood with legs spread and hands on his hips, like the captain of a naval ship in some old novel, lord of all he surveyed. With a nod from Mark, Kevin parted his lips, keeping his palms flat against his muscular thighs.

Mark slid his erection into Kevin's mouth. Unlike Kate, who would have begun to kiss and suckle her master at that point, Kevin stayed as still as stone. Mark arched his back until his cock was completely down Kevin's throat. Kevin's nose was pressed hard against Mark's pubic bone, buried in the lush black curls. Both men stayed perfectly still for over a minute, their eyes closed.

Kate felt a frisson of anxiety. Kevin needed to breathe! This must be what he meant by the "breath test". Kevin was expected to hold his breath, not to breathe until Mark decided that he should. What an ultimate submission! To have your very breath controlled by another. To trust your very life to your master. Could she do that? Would she panic and pull back? She liked to think she could do it, but if she were honest, she didn't know.

She watched now with fascination and concern, as Kevin's face reddened and his chest expanded with the effort to sustain his lungs. Finally, very slowly, Mark pulled back, allowing his "boy toy" to breathe. Kevin sucked in a huge breath, and was immediately impaled again by his master's cock. Over and over they played at this game, and Kevin never once faltered or showed any discomfort.

Kate moved in closer, watching as Mark's thick cock eased deep into her master's throat, and then was withdrawn, revealing the bulbous head, purple and shining with Kevin's saliva. After some minutes Mark pulled out completely, though he hadn't orgasmed.

"I seem to recall a playroom," he said to Kevin, who was wiping his face now on the back of his hand. His own penis still bobbed, fully erect, perpendicular from his belly.

"Oh, yes. And I have even more toys since you were here last." Since he was there last? Kate felt the prick of jealousy again. This man had been in Kevin's life for far longer than she. Who knew what intimacies they had shared, and none of them with her. Well, she was here now, and she knew that Kevin loved her. She would continue to try to submit with grace, and swallow any misgivings or fears.

Kevin released Kate's wrists, and together the three of them walked to the playroom, carrying their brandy with them. Mark had pulled his jeans back on, not bothering with underwear, but his two submissives were still completely nude.

Mark surveyed the room, his eyes lighting with pleasure as he took in the various instruments of sexual torture. The sturdy metal chair, with leather cuffs and thick shiny bands attached to the legs and arms, promised hours of fun at some poor submissive's expense, or pleasure, depending on your perspective.

He noted the array of whips and crops hung neatly along one wall and nodded, moving closer to inspect a particularly lovely red leather flogger with many soft suede tresses hanging invitingly down. There was a doctor's exam table, with the added touch of large flexible bands, which could be used to hold a person down at the chest, pelvis and ankles. In the ceiling were several sturdy hooks, handy for attaching chains or rope to secure one's slave during a whipping.

Mark stared at Kate then, his face registering some disapproval. "She could use some building up. More muscle. She's almost too thin, except for those great tits. I do admit…the tits are fantastic. Perfect for whipping." Kate looked down. She wasn't used to having her body criticized. Since she'd first begun to develop as a teenager, men had seemed to line up in order to ogle and adore her body. She was insecure in other ways, but not about her graceful form.

Maybe that was just his way of trying to gain the upper hand. Kevin never felt the need to put her down, but she knew some "masters" did it as a matter of course. The humiliation was a turn on for both parties. But Kate didn't like it. She tensed as Mark went on, "Have you ever secured her tits with those pretty chains? I'd like to see those nipples stretched, pulled taut till she screamed. Let's do that! Let's see what the cunt can take."

"Uh, no." Kevin's voice was firm, for the first time that evening. "I'm sorry, Mark, but no. The piercings are relatively new, and Kate's nipples are especially sensitive."

Mark bunched his lips, his displeasure evident on his face. Then he let out a sigh and said, "Fine. She's yours, after all. Though, if she were mine, she'd soon learn to tolerate a little 'sensitivity', I can assure you. I'd make her sleep with her nipples tethered to the headboard. If she so much as moved funny, she'd get a sharp reminder that those nipples were mine. Mine to torture, even to rip clean through if I wished."

Kate shivered, hugging herself, covering her breasts protectively. Silently she thanked her lover for not allowing Mark to secure her by her nipples! The very real concern of her nipple ripping from too hard a pull was a particular fear of Kate's and one that Kevin was aware of. When he'd convinced her to allow him to pierce her nipples, he'd promised he would never harm her, or use her unwisely. She remembered now how he'd kissed each nipple, still terribly tender from the needle, and promised her he would cherish her sweet little buds. She smiled slightly, remembering, and lightly touched the little gold rods that she now loved.

Kevin didn't respond directly to Mark, but instead moved toward Kate, draping his arm comfortingly around her. His erection had flagged, which Mark now noticed. Reaching down, he touched Kevin's cock, and lightly slapped his balls. "Relax, boy toy. I'm not going to harm your precious sub. Obviously, you're in love, and that changes things, doesn't it? Personally I find when love enters the equation, submission tends to go by the wayside, but what do I know?"

What indeed, Kate thought, deciding for certain now that she didn't like this man. But Kevin was still in his thrall, and she wanted to please and obey her lover. She would prove to this Mark that obedience and submission, coupled with love, could be more powerful than any S&M games he might play.

"I have a nifty idea," Mark said, his tone now playful. "I'm going to tie you two sluts together and whip you both! Two subs with one stone. What shall I use to bind you, boy toy?" Kevin got some rope from a chest, and handed it to Mark, along with a pair of small sharp scissors. Mark quickly cut several long pieces. He instructed the two of them to face each other, arms at their sides.

As Mark wrapped the thin, strong nylon rope around their thighs, and under their arms, high around their chests, the two lovers were forced close together, Kate's breasts pressed against Kevin's ribs, and his cock poking against her belly.

Mark stood back after a moment, surveying his handiwork. He was good with knots, and Kevin and Kate were tethered securely now to one another, waiting silently for their whipping. Mark selected the red leather whip, running the tresses through his fingers. He swished it through the air a few times, smiling a little as Kate winced at the sound it made as he flicked it in the air near her head.

Carefully Mark placed a sleep mask over each of his charges' eyes. Kevin sighed slightly, and Kate leaned her head against his chest, wondering just what was going through his head. She could feel his cock, hard now between them. He was turned on; he liked being tied up. Kate wasn't certain how this made her feel. It was exciting though, to be bound up to her lover, waiting for a flogging at the hands of another.

"Ah, the two lovebirds," Mark said, as he reached his hand between Kevin's legs, cupping his heavy balls. He moved his hand forward, finding Kate's shaven pussy. With a thick finger, he entered her, feeling her wetness. Kate drew in her breath sharply. Mark's fingers were thicker than Kevin's, and his touch less gentle. And yet, there was no denying his rough touch turned her on. She moved very slightly against his hand, resisting her impulse to grind wantonly against him.

Pulling his finger from the aroused girl, Mark dragged the wet digit across Kevin's ass, remarking, "Sluts, both of you. Subs are so easy. So fucking easy." He laughed, but there was affection in the laugh, and Kate tried to relax against her lover, mentally preparing for their whipping.

She loved when Kevin whipped her with the flogger, beginning with a sensual, slow lashing, barely more than a whisper of leather. Slowly he would work his way up and down her body, moving from her ass to her breasts, from her thighs to her back. He would cover her in sensual fire, slowly whipping her harder and harder, but never so hard that she couldn't bear it.

Sometimes, Kate would enter that lovely trance-like state of being where she truly did not distinguish between pleasure and pain, but only existed on some floating cloud of sensual ecstasy, hovering on the edge of orgasm, tethered to her lover by the lash, by her love and by their mutual desire. Unlike the trance she'd entered into earlier in the evening, the ones Kevin could induce in her could last for as long as an hour. Afterward she would be completely spent, a limp rag doll in his arms. Happiness would radiate from her like the sun.

Mark stood near the bound lovers, dragging the soft heavy tresses between his fingers. Kate felt his presence, and was actually eager for the gentle flick of those suede lashes. But Mark was not Kevin, and his whipping hand was not gentle. He had no desire to be sensual, or slowly arouse. For Mark there was no romance. Their pain was his pleasure.

When Mark first struck her, hard, she jerked against Kevin, unprepared. Why she had expected the same loving touch as Kevin delivered, she didn't know. She tensed, ready for the next onslaught. Mark walked in a slow circle around the bound pair, wielding his whip with an exacting and expert hand. Kate felt Kevin's cock rising hard against her as they were repeatedly thrust into each other from the blows. Her own pussy was wet, and their bodies were sweating against each other from the bare skin on skin.

Lost in the darkness of her blindfold, Kate gave herself over to the lash, savoring its hot kiss. Mark's style was different, but exciting. He was using them for his own pleasure. Torturing them because he got off on it. This wasn't all about Kate. She wasn't sure yet if that suited her, but really, she had no choice.

Her mind stilled as her body focused on his lash and when it would strike next. As he moved from body to body, lashing and striking at whim, neither would know where the next blow would fall. They would both jump a little, no matter which one was struck. It was almost as if they were one person, bound together, suffering together, under Mark's relentless onslaught.

Kevin's skin felt hot as fire to Kate. She could hear his breathing, labored, over her head. Her legs were tired and the brandy had left her woozy. Yet her pussy burned as the whip whistled and landed against their flesh, over and over again.

Finally, Mark dropped the whip. Kate felt his hands running up and down her flanks. He moved behind Kevin, no doubt doing the same thing to him. "So hot," Mark whispered, his voice hoarse. Mark released the knots of the ropes that held them. He pulled the masks from the two subs who squinted a little against the light. Their backs and asses were crisscrossed with the marks left by the whip.

"On your knees," Mark commanded, and Kevin and Kate dutifully sank to their knees. Kate was grateful not to have to stand anymore. Mark stepped out of his jeans, revealing again that thick, bulbous penis. He thrust it toward Kate, clearly expecting her to open her mouth and accept it. Was he going to choke her with it, impaling her as he had done to Kevin?

But no, he simply stood there, allowing her to lick and suckle it as she was used to doing for Kevin. Of course, Kate had had other boyfriends, other lovers, and had sucked other cocks before Kevin's. But how curious now to be doing this, and with her lover at her side! Mark's cock was so thick, with such a large head, that it was difficult for Kate to get her mouth around it.

She gamely tried, hoping she was pleasing the man, but somehow doubting it. After a few moments, Mark pulled his member from Kate's mouth and moved slightly so that he was now standing in front of Kevin.

Kevin's mouth opened like a little bird's, and Mark slid his penis in, again pushing forward to the pubic bone.

He looked down on Kate, his expression bemused, even disdainful, as if saying, there now, *this* is how you do it. Kate looked away, at once irritated and aroused.

"Can I fuck your sub, boy toy? Is that allowed?" Mark's voice was husky with lust, as Kevin's throat muscles held his penis tight. Unable to answer with his voice, Kevin nodded.

He was going to let this man fuck her!

Kate couldn't seem to catch her breath. This man with the huge cockhead was going to enter her. And Kevin not only would be there, but he had approved it, given his permission. Of course, he hadn't asked her if *she* would permit it; she had promised earlier to obey whatever he asked, no matter how outrageous. Really, she supposed, this wasn't unexpected. Most "swinging" couples exchanged partners, barely seeming to think about it.

But somehow she had Mark pegged in her mind as gay, with a capital G. That image didn't include him sticking his cock into her! "Get on your hands and knees, slut," Mark ordered. He crouched behind her, positioning his cock, still wet from Kevin's attentions, and pressed against her pussy.

Kate moaned, partially from pleasure, but also from pain. The head of his cock was so large he actually ripped the delicate flesh at her entrance slightly as he pressed into her. "Oh!" she cried out. But he held her hips, ignoring her cries, and the pain was quickly superseded by a heavenly hot melt of pleasure emanating from her sex and moving throughout her body.

Each thrust felt so good…so good. She bit her lower lip to keep from begging him not to stop. Vaguely she was aware of Kevin sitting in front of her, holding her still, as a way to participate in the taking of his woman, this ultimate submission on his part to Mark.

After several lovely minutes, Mark pulled back, popping out of Kate's sopping pussy. She couldn't stop the little sigh of dismay that escaped her lips. Mark heard it, and laughed. "I told you, boy toy. Easy. Any big cock will do for her; she just wants to be fucked. Don't you, whore? You just want to be fucked."

Kate colored, feeling the heat in her face and chest. She didn't answer, but what he said was true. She needed a big cock thrust up into her, and she needed it bad. But now she felt Mark's large cockhead pressing against her asshole. This was another kettle of fish entirely!

Kevin sometimes fucked her that way, but not very often, and while she submitted to it, she frankly didn't like it. The pain shadowed the pleasure too often for her, and she found it hard to relax. Secretly she was worried she might be "dirty" back there, and that this would turn off her lover.

Now she pulled forward, leaning into Kevin, her eyes silently beseeching him to intervene. Mark pressed again against her nether opening, and Kate squealed and then gasped, tensing. "Shit," Mark said. "Don't you ever use her ass? You got some KY or something to lube this damn virgin up?"

"Uh, Mark," Kevin said, "Uh, I don't know if that's a good idea."

"That's ok, boy toy. You don't have to know. I want to fuck your bitch in the ass. That's all you need to know. Do you have a problem with that?" He thrust harder against Kate, and she jerked forward, crying out.

"Uh, I'm sorry, Mark, but as a matter of fact I do. She isn't ready. Your cock, you know. It's hard for even the most seasoned sub to take. You'd rip her in half." The words might have been intended to flatter, but the underlying tone was clear.

Mark sat back, his expression sour. But Kevin's expression was resolute, and Kate felt tears of gratitude filling her eyes. Kevin may be submissive to Mark, but clearly, he placed his love for Kate, and his responsibility to keep her safe, above it.

Mark and Kevin stared at one another for a moment, and it was Mark who looked away first. Then a slow smile spread on his face and he said, "Okay then, boy toy. If you won't let me fuck her ass, you'll stand in as a substitute." Fingering his own thick, erect penis, Mark turned to the young woman. "Hey Kate, you ever watched two men fucking? You ever see your lord and master Kevin here get fucked in the ass by another man?"

Slowly Kate shook her head, her eyes wide. Would Kevin permit this? After all, he was taller by a good six inches and could easily overpower Mark if he chose. And yet she knew this wasn't about brute strength. Kevin could overpower her too if he wanted. No, it was about the free exchange of that power. The giving over of yourself—the submission.

And so she wasn't really surprised when Kevin bowed his head. Shifting up onto his knees, Kevin knelt up, locking his hands behind his back. His erection had wilted somewhat and Mark snapped, "Girl, get it hard."

Kate tried to catch Kevin's eye, seeking approval, but he was looking down submissively. She obeyed Mark, drawing her tongue along the sweet curve of her master's cock, feeling it stiffen in her mouth.

"Here's how I want to do this, subbies. You, Kate, lie down flat on the floor. I'm going to fuck your boyfriend on top of you. That's right, you're going to lie beneath us, and watch my cock thrust in and out of your lover's ass. Go ahead. What're you waiting for! Lie down!"

With a glance at Kevin, Kate lay down on the carpet. Even as soft as it was, it felt rough against Kate's tender flesh, newly whipped.

Kevin jumped up for a second, getting a tube of lubricant, which he handed to Mark before kneeling again, a knee on either side of Kate's supine body. He was kneeling so that she was upside down from him, her face under his ass, his face over her knees.

Mark knelt behind him, smearing a dollop of the ointment on his cock. Kate could see both men's balls, swinging over her head. She watched as Mark pressed his cock against Kevin's sphincter. Kevin grunted a little, and shifted his hands for more support, but otherwise didn't protest as Mark slid his greased penis into Kevin's ass. He was clearly no virgin.

Kate watched from below, fascinated. Kevin's ass was firmly muscled, the cheeks now neatly split as Mark's thick head pressed into him. Mark moved slowly, carefully. For all his bravura, it was clear he didn't want to hurt Kevin. Once he was fully in, however, he began to move with more insistence, pulling out and then thrusting back into Kevin's ass, his heavy balls swaying. Soon Mark was panting, grunting in his pleasure. Beads of sweat dropped onto Kate's body, but she wasn't sure whose.

Kate's eyes were wide as she watched Mark claim her man in this base and primal way. Her hands, free at last, slipped down to her own ignored sex, and she began to fondle and rub herself, breathing hard along with the two men, who were barely aware of her, lost in their own pleasure.

Kevin lifted a hand, grabbing his penis, massaging the shaft in long slow strokes as Mark fucked him from behind. Kevin's pace picked up in tempo to match Mark's. As Mark neared his own release, both men groaned, their heads back, Kate forgotten beneath them. Kate felt a spasm of white-hot pleasure. As debasing as it was to be underneath the two men, ignored and forgotten, or perhaps because of this debasement, Kate felt herself nearing her own delicious orgasm.

And yet, as Kevin's property, she wasn't permitted to come without his express permission. She didn't dare interrupt the two men, and so, reluctantly, she dropped her hand, aware that a few more strokes would invariably take her over the edge. Her heart was pounding, and the men above her were writhing and sweating, their grunts pure animal. Would they even notice if she took her own little pleasure?

It didn't matter, she suddenly realized. She didn't want to "steal" from Kevin, whether he knew or not. Her desire to submit didn't end when he couldn't see her. After all, she was alone all day while he was at work, and she had never, ever betrayed his command that she only orgasm in his presence, or at his express command. So, pussy still throbbing, Kate lay still under the two men.

A few more minutes of savage thrusting, and Mark shot his load, holding hard on Kevin's hips, pumping into him as he shouted, "Yes! Yes, you cocksucker! Take it, boy toy! Take it for me!"

Kevin began to spurt, his seed falling in hot little blobs over Kate's breasts and belly. Still on fire herself, she longed for the sexual release she was witnessing but still dared do nothing about it. In a curiously sweet gesture, given the brutal way Mark had just used Kevin, he wrapped his arms tightly around the taller man, resting his cheek for a moment against Kevin's back. It was Kevin who pulled away, rolling from his position over Kate's body. Mark sat back on his heels, his penis now dangling limply, his eyes on Kevin, who was leaning solicitously over Kate.

She sat up slowly, leaning on one elbow. She looked at the two men, one tall and blond, the other short and dark. Mark's eyes were blazing as he watched the two lovers. Kate found herself wishing he wasn't there any longer. Ignoring him by turning to Kevin she whispered, "Are you okay, baby?"

"I'm great," Kevin said, pushing his heavy curls from his forehead. "You're great. I love you, Kate." She kissed his cheek, tasting the salt of his sweat, pressing her thighs together to suppress her still unrequited sexual need.

"Man, it's a hundred degrees in here," Mark offered, drawing their attention back to himself. "Let's go take a swim, why don't we? And then have some of Kate's dessert? Or wait, let's have *Kate* for dessert!" He laughed at his own joke, and they all walked out to the pool.

The sky was black, pocked with silver pinpricks, and crickets and frogs added a symphony of summer sound. The water was warm, as Kevin kept the pool heated, even in summer, since he and Kate often took a dip on warm evenings. Kevin flicked on the pool lights, bathing the area in a warm glow. The pool was also lit from under the water, creating a hazy, magical effect.

The water felt wonderful, cooling Kate's hot, needy pussy, and soothing her still stinging back. She ducked under, swimming down to the end of the pool and back again, feeling free and strong, as she always did in the water. The men were leaning against the pool edge, sipping cold beers as they watched her. She came up for air, throwing her head back, flinging the water from her face with a toss of her head.

"Your little slut hasn't come yet, has she, Kevin? Should we leave her needy, or should we amuse ourselves?"

"You're the guest," Kevin grinned, now fully in control of himself again. "What's your pleasure?"

Mark snagged a large raft that had been floating nearby. "All right then. I'd like to see her play with herself. This time *with* permission."

Kate blushed, realizing that of course he had observed her hand, buried in her pussy, while he had been sodomizing her lover. Kevin looked at her quizzically, but didn't comment.

"Go on, girl. Climb up on this raft and show us what you can do. Entertain us. Make it sexy. No rough and dirty jerk off. Give us a show."

"Wait!" he shouted suddenly. "I have an idea!" Scrambling from the pool, Mark ran inside, dripping a trail of water as he went. A moment later, he returned, holding up a large flesh-colored dildo.

"One of my favorite toys," he grinned evilly. "Does your girl like implements?"

"She does if I tell her she does," Kevin assented. Mark handed her the dildo and walked back to the edge of the pool, standing close to Kevin.

Kevin held the long rope that encircled the raft, thus keeping the naked woman nearby. She held the large dildo for a moment, comparing it mentally to the two men.

Neither was as large as this thing; no wonder men had complexes about penis size! She wondered for a moment if she could accommodate such a large and unyielding phallus, but knew she had no choice. The men were waiting.

Remembering Mark's command for a "show", Kate slowly licked the rubber shaft, wetting it with her saliva. She placed it on her tongue and slid her head down, making a point to look up at the men with a coquettish expression, as if she loved taking this hunk of rubber down her throat.

They were watching, their beers forgotten, as she lay back on the raft and spread her legs. Pointing the dildo toward her pussy, she touched the tip of it to her entrance. Moaning a little, still just for show, she pressed it in, sliding it up into herself, and then withdrawing it slowly.

To her surprise and pleasure, it felt good! It wasn't Kevin, it wasn't even "Fatty", but it was something nice and hard, and it filled up an ache that had been building all night. Kate's eyes closed, and she forgot the men leering at her as she began to fuck herself in earnest. She held the dildo so that it could stimulate her clit as it slid in and out of her now wet pussy. Faster and faster she pumped it, writhing now with real pleasure as she felt the building of a sweet release.

At last, she was going to be allowed to come! Her moans had shifted to little pants, and she lifted her bottom from the raft to make better contact with the rubber cock. "Ungh, ungh, ungh," she cried, beyond awareness of anything but the shaft buried inside of her, riding her by her own hand to climax.

"Please!" she yelled, just in time remembering her place, and that she was always to ask Kevin for permission to orgasm.

"Yes!" Kevin shouted, completely absorbed in her performance, his cock again at full mast. Both men sighed as she slipped over the edge of ecstasy, coming hard at her own hand, the water splashing and sloshing over her raft as she shuddered and jerked with pleasure.

At last she stilled, the dildo still buried to the hilt in her pussy. Kevin swam over to her and gently pulled the item from her body. Kate opened her eyes and smiled blearily at him.

Mark, still standing at the side, began a slow clapping and said, "Applause for the slut. Good show, Kate. Very good indeed."

Kate sat up, suddenly feeling modest, and closed her legs. She slipped off the raft and wrapped herself around her lover. He held her and they moved together to the side of the pool. Mark said, "I could go for that dessert now. That *other* dessert."

Chapter Four

When Kate awoke the next morning, she reached over, as she always did, to find Kevin's warm strong body. Her hand met only the cool sheets. Eyes opening, she noted that her lover was not in the room. It was morning, but still early. She could tell by the way the sun slanted into the window, all pinks and buttery yellow.

Kate lay back, trying to recall the events of last night. They had all had plenty to drink — too much, in retrospect. Dessert had been accompanied by strong coffee, heavily laced with Bailey's Irish Cream. Now Kate's head pulsed slightly, and her mouth seemed to be full of bitter cotton. She reached for some Advil and swallowed several little pills with a large gulp of water.

Dimly she recalled that after the raspberry chocolate torte, the three of them had sat together, still naked, on the couch, she sandwiched between the two men, as they watched TV, drank more brandy, and fondled the girl between them.

Then it came rushing back, unfolding like a little video before her eyes. Whatever show they had been watching on TV was over, and Mark pushed the off button on the remote and stood up.

"Hey, Kevin," he said, grinning. "I haven't showed you my newest toy yet!"

"Oh, Mark and his toys," Kevin said to Kate, as if Mark were a little boy who had to be indulged. Mark got his toy bag and drew out a small slim briefcase. He clicked the little catches open and lifted the lid. Nestled in purple satin was a black rod of plastic, maybe twelve inches long. There were also several attachments that could be screwed onto the rod. Mark lifted a little glass globe and attached it to the rod. He plugged the device into the outlet next to the couch and flicked a little switch.

The glass globe looked to Kate like one of those electrostatic lightning sphere things they sold at Radio Shack or some such, only it was smaller, and on a handle.

"It's a violet wand!" Mark said triumphantly, grinning wickedly at them both. "Don't you know what that is?"

"I've heard of them, sure," Kevin said. "It's for 'shock' play. It's a play torture device. Used in the scene for party games. But aren't they dangerous?"

"No, no. Not if they're handled properly. They can be very intense, but not dangerous at all. The 'violet' part of the term comes from the little zaps of lightning. See?" Mark moved the wand closer to his own arm, waving the little hollow glass ball, which glowed with purple lightning inside. "See, it uses electrical sparks with an adjustable intensity to create a variety of sensations from a faint prickle to a bracing shock. Held near the body, it sends a continuous stream of tiny sparks. The combination of electrical stimulations is endless."

Kate's eyes were widening as she watched his display. This was like a cattle prod! She shrank back against Kevin, and clutched his arm. "We don't like that, do we, Kevin?" she whispered urgently.

Mark, who heard her, laughed and said, "Oh, Kate. Don't be such a wimp! Aren't you subbies supposed to be the courageous ones? The brave and obedient slave girl submitting to her master's pleasure? Or are you really just some kind of masochistic slut, who only accepts the so-called torture that makes you come? Huh? Which is it? Submissive, or just plain whore?"

"Mark. Stop it," Kevin said, his voice a warning. Then, "Of course Kate's submissive. She's the sexiest and bravest sub you'll ever meet. If I tell her to submit to that little wand, she'll do it with grace, won't you, love?"

Kate took a gulp of her brandy and set it down, none too steadily, on the low table in front of them. Now that Kevin had backed her into a corner with his compliments, she felt she had no choice but to nod, though her stomach was knotting in fear. The thought of electrical shocks was not erotic, merely frightening.

Mark nodded, his expression indicating he'd scored a point, though Kevin was a little too drunk to notice the nuance. Mark continued his lecture about his little toy. "You see it's quite innocent. The current doesn't travel through your body. It is more like a controllable static shock, but much more pleasurable. Kevin, hold out your arm. We'll show Kate how harmless this is." Kevin obediently held out his arm and Mark went on, "I'm using the largest globe attachment here. Its big size makes it the softest item in the kit." He turned a knob, lowering the intensity, and touched the glass ball to Kevin's arm. Slowly he moved the globe away. "You'll notice, boy toy, as the distance increases, the sensation felt increases as well, until the distance becomes too far and the arc is broken. This large globe is a great warm-up item since almost anyone can take it."

"It feels like a balloon," Kevin remarked. "Like the sensation when you rub a balloon on your arm."

"That's right," Mark agreed, smiling. "Though if I do this," he twisted the knob slightly and Kevin jerked, as the electric shock intensity increased, "It's got a little more kick than a balloon, doesn't it?"

"Yes," Kevin whispered. He licked his lips and shifted, but still held out his arm. Mark watched him carefully, and both men's cocks were now rising. He drew the glass sphere down Kevin's arm, along his chest, moving it closer and farther from Kevin's skin to vary the sensation. Kevin jerked slightly as the electroshock increased. Otherwise, he stayed still, except for his cock, which rose higher and higher.

"Yes," Mark said, "I thought it'd turn you on. Let's try on it on Kate, here. See what she can tolerate."

"Oh, no," Kate said, "I couldn't. I'm afraid of being shocked. I wouldn't like it."

"Katie, honey. It's sexy. I wouldn't let him do something I didn't think you'd like. He just did it to me. It feels like a prickle. Like a sexy kind of little jolt. It's hot, baby. You can do it. For me."

"That's right. He wouldn't *let* me do it, if it weren't safe," Mark said, his tone ironic, almost bitter. Kevin looked away and Kate felt the tension again between them. Part of her just wanted to go to bed, but she wasn't the one calling the shots. Though just who was calling them now, wasn't necessarily clear.

Hoping to ease the tension, Kate acquiesced. "Okay. I'll try it."

"Oh, goody," Mark said. "Now, the only way it's really fun is if we tie her down. Makes for more erotic tension." He paused a moment and then said, "How about that cool exam table? Let's tie her down there." Kate gripped Kevin's arm again, but he leaned over her, kissing her deeply, passionately. She eased her grip, and took another drink of brandy. She *did* like being tied down on that table. It reminded her of some kind of kinky James Bond movie, where she was the beautiful spy, caught in the villain's evil web, awaiting her rescue by Sean Connery — the only true Bond, in her book.

In the playroom, Kate was bound to the exam table, thick straps securing her comfortably but surely to the table just under her arms and at her waist. Her legs were free and now placed in the stirrups, which gave the two men an excellent view of her bare shaven sex.

To relax her, and perhaps also to subtly remind Mark who actually owned her, Kevin leaned down between Kate's legs and tongued her pussy for several moments. Her labia swelled under his expert kiss, and she sighed with lust, arching up toward him as best she could.

Meanwhile Mark circled her, holding his little wand, the purple lightning dancing in its globe. He brought the device close to her skin and she jerked a little. It didn't hurt; Kevin was right, it was like the electricity of a balloon on a winter's day, only more intense.

Kevin continued to lick her pussy, which kept her reasonably distracted while Mark moved his wand over her skin. He touched the metal of her nipple ring and that sent a jolt, which was no longer a tingle. It hurt! Kate screamed, jerking against her leather restraints. Kevin's head shot up and he said, "What happened?"

"Nothing, nothing," Mark said, his voice soothing. "Sorry, Kate. Guess it isn't a good idea to make contact with metal. I'll be more careful." Kate was breathing hard, but she wasn't really hurt. Startled was more like it, now that the shock had receded. She closed her eyes as Kevin again begun to suck and tease her wet pussy, sticking his tongue deep into her, his hands on either thigh.

"You can take this, can't you, Kate? It's hardly more than a kiss of electricity, right?" Mark asked, and, as Kate nodded he said, "Kevin. I want to try a different head. Something with a little more juice. She can take it. She's so *brave*."

Kate wanted to ignore the sarcasm in his voice. She *was* brave. She'd show the bastard. She didn't protest as Mark unscrewed the little glass globe and reattached another head. It looked like a small rake, with five tines.

Gently Mark dragged it across Kate's skin. She jerked and shuddered at the contact, feeling a series of tiny shocks spread over her nerve endings. Coupled with Kevin's kisses, and too much alcohol, Kate sank again into a sexual trance. Her eyes closed, she periodically jerked or moaned, pleasure and pain a confusion in her mind and body.

When Mark shifted the wand, so that only one tine touched her mons, just above Kevin's head, she was ripped out of her sexual reverie. The jolt was concentrated in that one little spot, and its shock lifted her out of the lovely blend of pleasure/pain and into just plain pain, which she registered with a scream, jerking in her bonds.

"Kevin!" she cried. "I want to stop! Let me up! I want to stop!" Kate and Kevin shared no "safe words" — those preplanned cues that were arranged between a Dom and his/her sub during BDSM play. Their friends in the scene all had safe words, things like "banana split" or "red light". But Kevin and Kate had always agreed that allowing the sub the ability to halt a scene like that was like cheating. It was for people who didn't know each other that well, or didn't trust each other implicitly, as they did.

For Kate, when she felt Kevin was taking her too far, she would simply say, "stop". And he would either stop, or he wouldn't, based upon his own decision as to what she could tolerate and how far he wanted to go. This suited Kate. Indeed, it heightened her arousal and made each submissive experience more exciting for her. Because she knew she could call out for him to stop, and he might, or he might not. It wasn't a game. She was truly at his mercy.

So this time, certain in her own mind that she needed to be released, that she couldn't tolerate the electric shocks any more and shouldn't have to, she called for him to stop. And she waited for him to kiss her, to murmur his reassurances and quickly release her.

Only he didn't. Was it the interplay between the two men? Was Kevin determined to show Mark that Kate, as his possession, could take whatever Mark cared to dish out? Or was it simply that he had had too much to drink, and wasn't properly gauging Kate's reaction, her very real level of fear.

Instead of releasing her, Kevin said, "Change the head, Mark. She doesn't like the rake. Try something different." Mark obligingly unscrewed the little rack and attached a mushroom-type of probe. He slid it across Kate's thighs, moving precariously close to her spread pussy.

Kate struggled in her bonds, crying out to Kevin that she was afraid. "She's a wuss, Kevin. She can't take it, not like you can. You're a better sub than your own sub. Guess you'll just have to take it for her, right boy toy?"

Mark stood behind Kevin, seeming to have lost interest in the squirming naked woman tied down to the table. He smoothed his hands up and down Kevin's back for a moment and whispered, "I'm going to use the rake on you, boy toy. I'm going to keep it up until you make her come. When she's done, you're done. Got it?"

Kevin nodded, dropping his hand down to stroke his own cock as he poised, his mouth over Kate's pussy, and his male lover crouched behind him. Mark raked Kevin's skin, varying the intensity of the shock play, sometimes causing Kevin to jerk forward against Kate's wet pussy, muffling a little yelp of pain. She didn't like having her master tortured. It didn't seem loving or sexy, as the play had earlier in the night.

She shut her eyes, giving in to his tongue and lips, wishing she hadn't had so much brandy, and wishing Mark would disappear. She realized she had better concentrate on her orgasm, and thus release her lover from the game.

When they finally let her up, it was only after Kevin brought her to an intense orgasm. At the moment of her climax, Mark raked the wand across the back of Kevin's neck, his eyes gleaming with sadistic pleasure.

Kate didn't recall much more. She had dim memories of being helped to bed, and kissed on the forehead by her lover, who told her he would be in soon. She fell into a brandy-laden stupor, not stirring until the morning, when she awoke to an empty bed.

And where were the "boys" now? Kate got up, used the toilet, brushed her teeth and splashed water on her face. She pushed back her heavy hair, now matted and smelling vaguely of chlorine, and thought she would like to shower. But she and Kevin always showered together, as part of their lovely morning ritual.

She went in search of him, pulling the silky little robe that he allowed her over her slender body. What she found at once repulsed and excited her. Her man and his guest were at the kitchen table, but not sitting side by side.

Instead, Mark was in a chair, the chair at the head of the table, which was normally Kevin's. He was wearing a black robe, but it was open, and his thick cock was sticking straight out. Kevin knelt at his feet, his mouth open as Mark slid a forkful of pancake into it.

Kevin chewed and swallowed. Then he moved his mouth to Mark's cock, which he dutifully took down his throat as far as he could from his position on the floor. He suckled it a moment, and then pulled back. Mark took a bite of pancake, offered another to Kevin, and so it began again.

Kate shifted against the doorframe, and the two men turned toward her. Kevin flushed slightly, but didn't move. Mark laughed and called to her, "Good morning, little cunt. Look where I've got your Master! Right on the floor, where he belongs, my cock in his mouth, him on his knees. And what does that make you, slave girl? Slave of the slave, eh?"

Kate stared at him, confusion rendering her mute. Slave of the slave? She didn't like the idea! Her master was slave to no one! And yet, the picture before her made a very clear statement to the contrary. Kevin was as submissive as she was, at least to this man.

"Drop the robe, slave," Mark commanded. Kate glanced at Kevin but he was suddenly occupied by Mark, who shoved his cock into Kevin's mouth holding him by the back of the head. Mark stared at Kate, as if to say, *I* am in command here. Look to *me*.

Kate dropped the robe, and Mark crooked a finger at her, gesturing for her to approach them. "Hungry, dear? Like a bit of cock with your coffee?" He let Kevin go and said, "Sit up, boy toy. Your replacement has arrived."

Kevin got to his feet. He was still flushed, but now Kate could see that his cock was as erect as Mark's. He took Kate in his arms, kissing her on the mouth. "Good morning, beautiful girl," he whispered. And louder, "Did you sleep well, angel? You pretty much passed out! No more brandy for you!"

Then gently he pressed her shoulder, and Kate obediently knelt before their guest. He began the same ritual, feeding her first a bite of food, and then his cock. She was struck again with the enormity of head and decided that Kevin's penis was much more beautiful, and more perfectly proportioned.

Kevin excused himself for a moment, and Mark seemed to suddenly tire of the game. "Sit at the table," he said brusquely. As she obeyed, he said, "So, just what are your intentions with Kevin?"

"Excuse me?" Kate wasn't sure she'd heard him correctly. The man sounded as if he was Kevin's father, and she was asking him for Kevin's hand in marriage. She smiled a little at the thought.

"I mean," Mark went on, not amused, "Do you think you're going to stick around here indefinitely? I should warn you, Kevin doesn't 'do' relationships. Oh, he's great at first, all lovey-dovey and very romantic. But take it from me," he leaned forward, lowering his voice, speaking quickly as if he knew Kevin might return at any moment,

"Kevin is commitment-phobic. Just like me. Women come and go in our lives, but it always comes down to us in the end. We were friends, and lovers," he paused meaningfully, as if expecting a response, but when none was forthcoming he continued, "long before you came onto the scene, little miss. I'm just warning you for your own good. So you don't get too attached."

Kate stared at Mark for a moment. She had not expected this! The man was warning her off! She felt as if they were in high school, and another girl was telling her to keep to watch out, and stay away from her guy. But this was no high school girl, and Kate had no intention of backing off, despite Mark's promise that whatever she and Kevin had wouldn't last.

The nerve of the man! Even as she bridled, Kate realized with compassion that Mark felt threatened by her. Perhaps this was the first time the dynamic was different between them, since the ingredient of love, love between Kevin and a woman, had been thrown into the mix. Mark obviously hadn't been counting on this. Perhaps he was in love with Kevin himself! The idea was a strange one, but would explain his behavior somewhat.

Kate considered taking Kevin aside and confiding what Mark had just said. He came back into the kitchen a moment later, bringing some fresh flowers from their garden, and looking very proud of himself. She didn't have the heart to ruin his day, and decided she might seem jealous or petty if she brought up Mark's peculiar comments. Better just to let it go. After all, he would be leaving soon.

After breakfast, as Kate was washing the dishes, the two men sat at the table, still sipping cups of hot coffee. "Unfortunately, I have to leave by lunchtime," Mark was saying. "But that still gives us a couple of hours to play, boy toy. I have a few wicked ideas in mind."

"I'm sure you have," Kevin grinned back.

Kevin was wearing cutoff denim shorts. He looked incredibly sexy as he lifted some free weights for Mark in the exercise room. Mark was openly admiring Kevin's firm pecs, his hand trailing across the taller man's chest as he strained to lift the two hundred pounds of metal over his head.

Kate stood nearby, naked save for the cuffs on her wrists, ankles and neck. She found herself feeling proprietary toward Kevin, wishing she could brush Mark's hand away. But after breakfast, while they were in the shower, Kevin had told her he wanted her to continue to obey Mark.

"It's weird," he'd admitted to her. "Something's definitely changed between us. I guess it's because of you." When Kate started to protest, Kevin hurried to explain, "No, I don't mean it's your fault or anything. Not at all! In fact, you've behaved wonderfully, really you have, darling. You've submitted with grace and courage, even to things I know you weren't comfortable with. If it's possible, I am more in love with you than ever."

Kate smiled, mollified, as Kevin continued. "I think what I mean is, something Mark said. He said, 'when love enters the equation,' it changes things." Kate recalled that this wasn't precisely what Mark had said, but she didn't correct Kevin. "And it's true," he went on. "Me and Mark have messed around over the years, maybe a dozen times. And it's always been fun. Just fun. Not this weird underlying tension I know we're all feeling from time to time this weekend. I think, this may sound odd, given how cocky and self-assured Mark is, but I think he may be jealous. Not of you per se. I'm not saying he's, like, in love with *me* or anything like that. I mean that he's jealous of what we have together. You and me.

"I can't recall Mark ever having a long-term relationship with anyone. He dates and stuff, and plays the field, but I don't even know if he's capable of committing.

"Maybe it has always worked so well between us because for so long I think I was the same way. We've played before with a woman, usually my girlfriend at the time, but it's never *mattered*. She was always—I know this sounds fucked up—but she was always *incidental*. She didn't matter for her own sake. That sounds really callous, I know it does. And I guess it was."

He looked down at Kate, perhaps trying to gauge if she understood what he was trying to say. She leaned into him, pressing her wet cheek against his chest. The hot water sprayed them soothingly as Kevin went on. "Now suddenly Mark's encountering a whole new thing with me. I'm in love. And he knows it. And I won't let him do whatever he wants. Because it's about you. You not only aren't incidental, you're my major focus—my major concern. I love you, Katie."

"May I ask a question? A blunt question?" Kate knew she was probably treading on dangerous ground now. There were things between her lover and Mark that she obviously didn't understand.

"Of course, Kate. Always."

"Well, do we have to go on? I mean, can't we just tell Mark it's been real, see ya? Do we have to keep submitting to him?"

Kevin pulled back from her. "Kate! Aren't you having fun? I mean, I know he's different from us. We're romantic, and he's just in it for the sex. But don't you think it's hot? Hey, you were the one who was always asking me about my gay experiences! You were the one who said it was hot to imagine me and some other guy getting it on right in front of you!

"Now your fantasies have come true, right? I mean, haven't they? Or," his face darkened suddenly, and his eyes opened with worry, "or did it really disgust you? And you no longer love me, or want to obey me, because I'm bi? You always knew I was bi, Kate. I told you from the beginning. You knew I'd been with guys. I believed you when you said that was cool—that was sexy. Now you're telling me it turns you off?"

"No! No!" Kate hurried to deny it. "Not at all. It *is* sexy. It's not that, please! It's just, well. It's Mark. There's something off about him. I don't know. Maybe…"

She paused, wishing she had never brought this up. Maybe she was just being insecure. She was used to having Kevin all to herself. Mark was so self-confident, and they'd shared years of closeness before she had ever come onto the scene. Maybe she *was* jealous!

Kevin scowled, "Oh, come on, Kate! He just had too much to drink last night. I should tell you, we were a lot more intense back then than you and I are. We were more into the pain, less into the erotica. He's used me a lot harder than you've seen so far. I used to really get off on it.

"I've just found that now, in a loving relationship with you, I feel right as your Dom. As the one in control. And with Mark, I feel right as his sub, as his boy toy. But please don't be jealous. Please do understand, with me and Mark, it's about the game, not about each other. To tell you the truth, I don't even *like* him that much. But I dig what we do together. It's intense. Do you see now?"

She didn't. Oh, she understood he got a thrill from the intense games Mark played. But she didn't understand how he could want to continue to play with someone who made her uncomfortable.

At that moment, a rift opened between them. It was silent but insidious, like a crack along the ice of a frozen lake. Kate felt it, like something cold ripping inside of her.

But she said nothing. Looking up at her handsome man, his face so earnest and open, so eager for her to accept just what he said at face value, she swallowed her misgivings and smiled up at him, the hot water running down her face like tears.

He kissed her, and she kissed him back, sliding down his body as she slowly knelt, taking his cock into her mouth and kissing it until it expanded and hardened against her lips. Teasingly she drew his member into her warm mouth and licked and swirled her tongue against it until she drew a moan from her man. She didn't stop until he came, shuddering, in her throat.

"Oops," he said, laughing. "I wasn't supposed to do that! Standing rules when I play with Mark are I only come in front of him. I've been a bad boy."

"I won't tell," Kate said, secretly feeling triumphant, as if she'd stolen something from Mark. She had been overreacting, she was sure of it. Mark wasn't a bad guy. Not her type, but there had definitely been some seriously sexy moments between them. It obviously excited Kevin to have Mark there, and she did acknowledge that it had been hot watching the two men fucking, and she'd enjoyed her own little exhibition in the pool.

Yes, overall, it felt wrong. But it wasn't like he was moving in or anything! He was leaving that very day. It made Kevin happy to have the guy around, an old friend from the past. A reminder of his wild college days, perhaps. And today they wouldn't be drunk like last night, so surely things would go better.

Most importantly to Kate, Kevin clearly wanted this. As they dried off, he said, "Remember, Mark is still your master, until he leaves. You will obey him, and whatever he says goes, as long as I don't protest. He can get a bit out of hand sometimes, but I think he's pretty clear about the ground rules now. You ready, sexy?" Kevin slipped a finger into Kate's silky sex. She moaned, pressing against him, loving the feel of him inside of her.

As he moved the finger, knowing just how to drive her wild, he kissed her. Pulling back, he whispered, "Make me proud, slave girl."

Chapter Five

Kate watched her man, sweating and heaving, as Mark touched him, letting his hands glide over the slick torso of her lover. "Put it down," Mark commanded. As Kevin carefully lowered his weights, Mark turned toward Kate. Pointing to the exercise cycle in the corner, he asked Kevin, "What about forced exercise? I do remember some lovely sessions. You with sweat dripping from your chin and biceps, your lovely blond hair matted and wet, your face a study in pain."

"No," Kevin admitted. "I haven't trained Kate like that. She's so thin I'd be afraid to wear her down to nothing."

"Nonsense. It'll build her up! She could use a few more muscles. Let's put her on the cycle. I love to see sweat beading up between a woman's breasts, trickling down her body. Like some kind of wild animal in heat."

"Well, if you really think so," Kevin hesitated, but then agreed, "Okay. Kate. Go show the man you're no wimp. Go ahead. Set it to high."

Kate obediently climbed onto the padded seat. It was long and narrow, and if she sat just so, it rubbed on her clit and made her hot while she peddled. Kate was no stranger to exercise, and though Mark may insult her and say she looked scrawny, she was in fact quite strong.

Now she set the bike to the lowest gear ratio, maximizing the resistance. Leaning forward, she began to peddle, aware of her breasts, with their pretty gold loops, hanging forward and jiggling as she rode. The men watched her quietly for a moment and then Mark said, "While she's working up a nice sweat, I can't wait to try out that cool chair." Turning toward Kate, Mark admonished, "Don't stop. When I come back I expect to find you've worked up a decent sweat."

He and Kevin left the naked girl to her task, and went into the playroom. Kevin sat down in what was called the "devil's chair". It was fashioned of black leather, polished to a shine, pulled over a sturdy metal frame. The chair had belts and cuffs to prevent the captive's arms, legs and torso from moving.

Kevin sat willingly, allowing Mark to strap him down, leaving his cock, of course, completely exposed. Mark buckled him securely, and then knelt down between Kevin's legs. Gently he cupped Kevin's balls in one hand, while lightly kissing and licking his cock until it swelled to a full erection. Without Kate there to impress, he seemed less domineering, more of a lover than a master. Slowly he opened his mouth, and took Kevin's long thick cock—all of it.

As he had taught Kevin, he stayed perfectly still, his windpipe blocked by Kevin's member, his own face pressed against Kevin's pubic bone. Slowly he withdrew, and then repeated the exercise. Kevin moaned and sighed as Mark rubbed his hands along Kevin's cock, and gently teased and tickled his balls.

When Kevin was breathing hard, clearly about to orgasm, Mark pulled away completely and stood up, a wicked gleam in his eye. "Want to come, don't you, boy toy?"

Kevin nodded, saying huskily, "Please, Sir, let me come."

Mark stood up, leaning over the bound man and slapped him across the face. Kevin's head jerked to the side, and his eyes widened. Mark leaned over and kissed him, hard, on the mouth. He stood back grinning, his eyes on Kevin's cock, which was bobbing almost parallel to his flat stomach. It was obvious from Kevin's reaction that he was turned on by what Mark was doing.

"Let me come," he whispered again, the need plain in his face.

"What, don't you want to come in your *lover's* mouth?" Mark spat the word lover out like it was an epithet. "Oh wait, I forgot. She's in the other room, humping the bicycle seat while you're here, all tied down. You couldn't get away even if you wanted to, could you, boy toy? You truly are at my mercy right now, aren't you?"

Kevin nodded slowly, his eyes bright. He was still aroused, but an edge of confusion, of doubt, was at last entering the equation for him. His penis flagged slightly and Mark noticed. He slapped at Kevin's cock, and said, "Keep it up, boy, or I'll whip that thing until you bleed." He slapped Kevin's penis again, harder. Kevin yelled, and started to protest, but Mark put his hand gently over Kevin's mouth.

Dropping to his knees again, he smiled up at Kevin. Then he kissed and licked the penis he'd just struck. Softly he said, "There, there, sweetheart. I'm just playing. You used to let me do anything, remember? Now suddenly there are all these rules. That girl in there has you bewitched, doesn't she? You're not my boy toy anymore, are you, Kevin?"

"Oh, Mark. Please. Kate and I are in love. You know that. That doesn't mean you and I can't still have fun from time to time. I think you should let me out of this thing now. Come on." Kevin's voice was calm, but there was an underlying insistence and perhaps a soupcon of panic.

Mark looked sharply at him, a spark of anger igniting in his eyes. But he hid it quickly, as he smiled again. "Yeah, I know. You're actually growing up, I guess. Something I don't know if I'll ever do. Not at least as measured by *committed relationships*." Again, the sneer was evident in his tone, and Kevin shifted nervously.

"Hey Mark, buddy. Let me out of this now. Let's go check on Kate."

"Oh yes, let's check on Katie-poo. See if she's come yet from fucking the bike seat."

"Mark." Kevin's tone was warning. This wasn't funny anymore.

"I'll go check on her, *buddy*. You just sit tight." Mark laughed a little, as it was obvious Kevin had no choice.

He entered the exercise room, and Kate had indeed worked up a sweat. She was breathing hard, and the cycle wheels were just a blur as her feet spun round and round. Her body shimmered with sweat, and as he watched, a large bead of perspiration slid from her chin, dropping down between her breasts.

"Aren't you a pretty picture," Mark breathed. "So hot. Literally and figuratively. Makes me want to throw you down and fuck you right there. Slip my cock in that slippery little naked cunt of yours."

Kate didn't like his tone. Where was Kevin? Without being told she could, Kate stopped pedaling and said, "Where's Kevin?"

"Oh, he's a little, uh, detained right now. In the playroom. He said we should go on ahead without him."

Kate got off the bike, her legs wobbling slightly, her muscles completely fatigued. She wiped her brow with a backhand gesture, and shook her heavy auburn hair from her face. "Where's Kevin?" she said again.

"Silly girl, I told you. He's in the playroom. Oh, all right, we'll go in there," he said, as Kate's face hardened. "Jesus, are you guys attached at the fucking hip or something?"

They entered the playroom and Kate saw her man, tethered securely in the devil's chair, the chair he would sometimes lock her into, leaving her completely exposed to his sweet tortures.

When Kevin put Kate in the chair, he would secure her legs wide open. Invariably he would begin with a slow, ticklish tease, sometimes using a feather to heighten the sensation all over her body. Sometimes he would lightly whip her thighs and her bared pussy, watching with pleasure and rising lust as her sexual juices started to flow, evidencing her arousal along with her cries of pleasure.

The "torture" would usually end with Kevin dropping to his knees and tonguing and licking her until she screamed for mercy. One favorite tease was to bring her to the edge, over and over, but deny her release. Her body would be shivering, shuddering, so close, and he would stop. Over and over, he knew just how far to take her until at the end she would literally be crying in frustration, desperate to come, desperate for release. When he would finally relent, not stopping as her body shuddered and her cries became a keening litany of need, she would climax so hard that sometimes she actually passed out with the intensity of her orgasm.

How odd to see her master there, himself naked and bound with thick strips of leather at his chest, wrists, thighs and calves. Mark pushed Kate further into the room. "Look at Kate, Kevin. She's worked up quite a sexy sweat, wouldn't you agree?"

Kevin nodded, smiling at Kate, his cock rising from its half-mast position. "Kevin, would you like to see me whip your slave girl? I'll use the crop. That cute little crop over there." He pointed to the long slender crop positioned midway up the wall. It was black, with a shiny rectangle of leather at one end, ideal for slapping a well-rounded bottom.

"I've never seen anyone give Kate a proper cropping," Kevin said. "But why don't you let me out of this first, Mark? I can help hold her still if that should become necessary."

"Oh, no, boy toy. You're not getting out of there so soon. I haven't had my fun with you yet. No. I can handle this little girl all by myself just fine, thank you." If Kevin sensed the unspoken challenge in the words, he said nothing. Perhaps he decided it would be humiliating to Mark not to let him have his way yet again. Mark pointed to the crop.

"Go get it, slave, so I can use it on your ass. Hurry up." With a glance at Kevin, not caring if this irritated Mark, Kate walked forward. Kevin had nodded to her, and smiled reassuringly. He must know what he was doing, she reasoned silently. And anyway, this man would be gone out of their lives in an hour or two.

She got the crop and handed it to Mark. "I need some water," she said to him. She was still sweating slightly, and she felt very thirsty.

"After your whipping, sugar. Then you can have all the water you want. Right now, bend over, and show me that gorgeous ass."

Kate obeyed, offering her sexy ass for the crop. Mark had positioned her in front of Kevin, so he had a perfect view of her bottom, and her sweet little labia peeking from the other side, looking very inviting indeed.

Mark started lightly, swatting first one cheek and then the other. Over and over he hit her, in a steady rhythm, until the only sound in the room was Kate's labored breathing and the sound of leather on skin. She felt dizzy, from the intensity of the whipping, and also from her thirst. She swayed a little, and Mark grabbed her wrists with one hand, as if to steady her. While he was the same height as she, he was much stronger, and his hands were much larger. He pulled her hands out and away from her body, forcing her to splay her legs to keep her balance.

"Please," Kate managed to whisper. Mark didn't seem to hear her. "Please," she said again, not quite daring to articulate that she needed him to stop. She didn't want to shame Kevin. Mark was very skilled with the crop, creating just enough sting to turn her on, without upsetting the delicious erotic balance between pleasure and pain. But she was thirsty, and still a little hung over from the night before. And she didn't like to see her man, bound and helpless as he was, in the devil's chair. She wanted to lie down. With Kevin. Alone.

"Please," she whispered again, this time directly beseeching Kevin.

Kevin finally intervened, saying, "That's enough, Mark. She's had enough."

Mark turned on him suddenly, his face tight, his eyes wild. "Oh, that's enough, huh? Boy toy is now ordering me around again? This whole fucking weekend you've stopped me at every turn. What the fuck has happened, Kevin? When did you become this cunt's little lapdog?"

"That's *enough*!" Kevin shouted. "Let me out of this right now. The game is over, Mark. You've definitely crossed the line."

"Oh, it's over, is it? I think I recall I'm the one who says when it's over, *boy toy*. You're not exactly in a position to protest, are you?"

Kate stood slowly, forgotten for the moment, watching this exchange with growing horror. Mark must have lost his mind! She hurried over to Kevin, aiming to unbuckle his wrists first. But Mark was too quick for her.

"Oh, no you don't, bitch!" Mark grabbed Kate from behind, pulling her away from Kevin. She screamed but he was too strong for her. "Not yet. I'll let him out, but not yet!"

Mark held Kate with one arm while he pulled his jeans down with the other. He kicked them away, still holding the struggling girl in his arms. Kevin was roaring now, shouting that Mark had better let him the fuck out or he would answer for it later.

"Oh, shut up, Kevin, you're so fucking tedious. I didn't know this bitch had turned you into some old school marm, for God's sake. Just shut up!"

Mark grabbed Kate's leather-cuffed wrists, forcing them behind her. He quickly clipped them together, and then pushed her to the floor. Grabbing her ankles, he did the same thing. Then he forced a gag between her teeth, silencing her protests to a muffled cry. As she lay struggling on the floor, he approached Kevin, who jerked against his leather restraints, hurling curses at Mark.

Mark took another ball gag from his "bag of tricks" and secured it around Kevin's head. Kevin tried to protest, but he could do nothing. Once he was gagged, Mark stepped back, satisfied.

"There, now maybe you'll shut the fuck up." Kevin's eyes were blazing with rage, and something else. Fear. He must have realized he'd placed Kate in a terribly dangerous situation. She was now at the mercy of a man he had thought he could trust. Somehow, what was supposed to have been a wild and fun weekend had gone horribly awry. And Kate! She had tried to warn him, and he had silenced her, convinced it was only jealous love.

Instead of listening, really listening, to Kate's genuine misgivings, he'd treated her as less important than himself. He'd allowed his own pride, and his own wishful thinking that things could stay as they had once been, to cloud his reason. And now his love might be in actual danger! And he couldn't even seem to talk Mark out of this, talk him "down" from this temporary insanity, if that was what it was.

Perhaps there had been more between them than he had realized. Perhaps while he had thought they were only playing, it had meant more to Mark. Perhaps Mark felt betrayed and humiliated. Whatever he felt, something had clearly snapped in that brain of his, and Kevin was forced to watch the scene that unfolded.

Mark approached Kate, who was writhing, trying to kick him as he approached. Mark reached for the nipple rings, jerking her roughly by each chain. Kate stilled immediately, terror now showing in her face, mingled with pain.

"That's right, Katie-poo. I thought that would calm you right down. Now here's what's going to happen. I'm going to fuck you in the ass with my nice big cock. Kevin here is not in a position to intervene this time, and I'm going to show you what it feels like to be used like a man. Like I used *your* man."

As he spoke, Mark forced Kate up on her knees. Because her hands were bound behind her, she was forced to take her weight on her forehead as Mark pressed her forward, straddling her legs from behind.

Taking a thin chain, he slipped it quickly through each chain at her nipples and drew it tight, holding the ends in his hands. He pulled on it slightly, demonstrating to Kate that if she moved suddenly, or if he chose to jerk it, the chains would tug the little bars in her nipples, hurting her or possibly worse. "That's right," he said, "You are now aware of your position, huh? I can rip those rods right out if I want to. Don't worry; I won't, as long as you behave yourself. As long as you let me fuck your little butt hole. Which I'm going to do, right now."

Kevin was straining in his chair, his face red, tendons standing out on his neck. He was past trying to understand what was going on in Mark's head, trying to put himself in Mark's shoes. Kate was being frightened and humiliated. She was going to be raped! Not the sexy fantasy rape that was in actuality consensual, but a brutal assault, a taking of something held dear. A betrayal of trust.

Kevin's face was a study in impotent rage. It was clear, if he could have gotten free at that moment, Mark would be a dead man. Instead, Kevin was forced to watch as Mark lubed up his penis, and pressed the bulbous head against Kate's nether hole.

She pulled away at first, but quickly stilled as Mark jerked on the chain, pulling the nipple chains hard against her. Kate squeezed her eyes shut, submitting to an anal rape that her lover was forced to watch. Tears were dropping from her face onto the carpet, but she no longer cried out, instead biting hard against the rubber lodged in her mouth, trying to keep as still as she could.

Even while being forcibly sodomized, she was thinking of her love. She didn't dare look over at him, fearing she would burst into fresh tears, and upset him all the more. She knew this must be sheer torture for him to watch what was taking place. She clearly understood the difference between their consensual exchanges of power and this act of violence.

She promised herself silently to just get through it, and somehow get away from this horrible man. She would call the police, and they would have him arrested for rape.

Mark pressed against his captive again, this time entering her. Kate involuntarily screamed against the gag, a gurgle of pain, as he forced his way past the ring of muscle and into her ass. In and out he slid, tugging lightly at the chain every so often to remind her of her place.

Mark was grunting, his body hot and sweating against hers. Each time he slammed into her, Kate's forehead shifted against the rug, burning her skin. Her hair was wild about her face, now blocking her view of her bound lover, even if she'd dared to look at him.

After a few minutes, Kate actually felt the pain ease. Her body was accustoming itself to the invasion, and she knew if she could just keep still and take it, it would soon be over. Mark rutted hard against her now, moaning and grunting like some kind of wild thing. Finally, he shot his load deep inside of her and slammed against her, accidentally pulling the chains taut, drawing one last squeal from Kate, which was muffled against the ball wedged into her mouth.

Mark pulled out of her, leaving a trail of his semen along her thigh. He stood up, watching as Kate fell to her side, still bound hand and foot. He looked at Kevin, his eyes wild, his breathing labored. Quickly Mark looked away.

Lightly he said, "Well, it's been fun, kiddies. Sorry you forgot what submission is about, boy toy. I don't suppose we'll be seeing one another again. That will probably be too soon for either one of us." He stared down again at Kate, who, like a cornered animal, was lying very still, where she had fallen, as if hoping he wouldn't notice her any more.

Mark pulled on his jeans and left the room, leaving them both bound and gagged. Kate wriggled furiously. The fucker was going to get away! She wanted to call 911 and have him arrested!

As she struggled against her cuffs, reality began to set in. The police would arrive, and see their playroom, and the whips and chains. They would never understand the huge difference between a loving and voluntary exchange of power, and the rape that had just taken place. They would probably end up arresting all three of them!

As these thoughts tumbled through her mind, Kate heard the front door open and then slam. Well, please God, he was gone! Now she just had to get herself free! She twisted, moving until she could see Kevin. He was still straining in his chair. The poor man was going to give himself a stroke! His face was covered in tears, and Kate's heart broke at that moment.

What had they done, letting that man into their lives? She lay still for several minutes, willing her heart to slow its beat. Her wrists were touching, and she could move her fingers. Slowly she reached up, trying to contort her fingers enough to reach the clasp that bound her cuffs.

At last, she touched it, and tried to slide the mechanism open. It took several tries, but finally the clasp was released and she was able to slide the ring through it and she was free! Reaching up with trembling hands, she unbuckled the gag from around her head and flung it from her.

"Oh, Kevin! Oh God, Kevin! Are you okay, baby?" Her voice broke in a sob. Quickly releasing her ankle cuffs, Kate ran over to the bound man and unbuckled his wrists. She removed the offending gag from his tear-streaked face with trembling fingers, and then released his bound torso and his ankles.

"Kate, oh, Kate, sweet Kate." Kevin was crying in earnest now, as was Kate. They stopped trying to comfort each other with words, and instead staggered out of the playroom, their arms around each other.

Kevin gently forced Kate to the couch. "Just sit there, please, darling. I'll just make sure that bastard is well and truly gone. And then I'll get you a bottle of water." At the mention of water, Kate's thirst flared up again in full force. Fear had made her forget her bodily needs.

He came back a moment later, a cold bottle of water in his hands. He sank down next to her and whispered, "I'm sorry. I'm so, so sorry." He broke down, sobbing, his head in Kate's lap. She stroked his blond curls, murmuring as she would to a child frightened in the night.

Chapter Six

Several months had passed. Mark's betrayal had left them frightened and scarred. They found to their sad surprise that they had become shy of one another. Kate found that while she still loved Kevin, she was no longer sure that she trusted him. That she trusted herself to submit to him. To give of herself so completely and openly as she had done before that fateful weekend.

They had never heard from Mark again. Both she and Kevin agreed it was best to be completely rid of him. They didn't plan to seek him out, or press charges. Kevin said over and over that they were well rid of him; he'd never dare to show his face again. He knew Kevin would kill him.

Kevin had begged Kate's forgiveness, and she had readily given it. After all, Kevin was guilty only of bad judgment. He'd certainly never meant to hurt her, or put her in harm's way. She truly did forgive him.

But she couldn't forget.

They talked endlessly at first about what had happened, what had gone wrong. Time became demarcated, defined as "before Mark" and "after Mark". Kate resented how he still controlled their lives, even after so many weeks had passed.

The cuffs she had worn as a proud symbol of her submission had been removed after the struggles with

Mark had chafed and burned her wrists. They still lay, unused, in her nightstand.

The lovely nipple rings, which had been such a source of pride to Kate, had become symbols of her fear. She would awaken night after night, horrible dreams of Mark ripping the rings from her flesh, or shocking her along the gold bars, jolting her to death with a huge cattle prod.

Kevin had finally removed them for her, telling Kate he didn't want her to suffer from her memories or her fears. One day, perhaps, she would wear the jewelry again. But it would be because she wanted them, not because Kevin demanded it. She was grateful for this gesture, and the dreams actually did ease, coming less and less often, and seizing a weaker hold each time.

At first, their lovemaking was tentative, careful. Kevin's kisses were hesitant, as if he expected a rebuff. And Kate was shy, wishing only to withdraw and retreat into the safety of being alone. She never openly refused him, but her body would close, like a flower that shuts itself off at night, drawing in on itself for protection.

And yet, they still loved one another. Kate had thought about moving out. About giving up her life as a "kept" slave girl. She had money saved, plenty to get herself on her feet again if she chose to return to the workaday world and live on her own. Yet she found she didn't want to leave. Though they no longer lived as master and slave, she cared deeply for Kevin. Indeed, she loved him. She just wasn't ready to go back to what they had.

And instinctively Kevin seemed to understand that if he wanted his darling girl back, he needed to give her time. At first, he openly cursed himself to her, going over the events again and again, trying to understand how he, himself, could have been so blind, so clueless, as to Mark's unsound mind and dangerous jealousies.

Kate begged him to stop, hating to watch the man who had once been her dominant lover metaphorically on his knees to her.

Slowly, they healed.

Slowly, their kisses, at first chaste, almost like those of brother and sister, heated. If their minds were occupied with the trauma Mark had visited upon them, their bodies still remembered each other's curves. The sweet, hot feel of Kevin's cock swelling against her in the night. The cool, lovely curve of her breast, the nipples dripping with pearls of water in their shower.

Slowly, they touched. At first hesitant, too careful. But then their bodies began to rediscover one another. To rediscover the merge of heated skin, the kiss of tongues entwining. His hands sought her delicate wrists, raising her arms high over her head as he claimed her, carefully at first, then less so, with his cock.

Slowly, they remembered. Kate remembered the sweet thrill of submitting to another's command. Sinking to her knees, opening her mouth like a baby, ready for the milk of his cock. Gathering courage from her willingness, her neediness, Kevin began to take what she offered, to demand just a little more.

What had been so lighthearted before Mark, now was serious, but also more special. It was fragile, but contained a promised strength.

A cold winter's night found Kate kneeling naked in front of the fireplace. Kevin had lit the logs and the flames crackled, flinging orange color around the room. Candles placed here and there offered an additional soft light, and the sweet scent of sandalwood.

It had been so long since they'd interacted as master and slave. Kate wanted to be here now, naked and kneeling. Kevin hadn't asked her permission. It would have ruined it if he had. That evening when he'd come home from work, she'd been kneeling naked at the door, just as she used to do, before Mark.

This was the first time. Kevin had remarked upon it when she'd stopped waiting at the door for him, but not as a rebuke. Instead of coming home to his naked submissive angel, waiting with bowed head and wet pussy for him, he would find her curled up on the couch perhaps, reading a book, or out in the garden, tending her beautiful flowers.

He never demanded that she return to her position and await his arrival, as she once had, a whip at her side. His eyes were sad, but his smile true when he promised her that he understood, and would wait for her. She was grateful for the reprieve, and almost felt that she was betraying their unspoken agreement by no longer submitting sexually to him.

Yet, she had promised herself that from now on she would honor her instincts. Perhaps if she'd been more open about her misgivings with Mark, things wouldn't have progressed as they had. Submission did not equal passivity. They had both learned this lesson well.

Now she knelt, naked, head down, her lovely hair tossed in waves, obscuring her bowed head. "Kate," Kevin had breathed, dropping his briefcase. She stayed silent, perfectly still, waiting for his cue. She felt his hand lightly upon her head and stood slowly, unwinding her long graceful body, holding up her face for his touch.

Gently he took her head in his hands and they kissed like new lovers, exploring and reacting with pleasure and delight. Then Kevin saw the whip nearby. The pretty red flogger they hadn't touched since before Mark. Indeed, neither of them had wanted to even enter the playroom these past months. But she must have gone in there to get this.

Pointing to the heavy flogger, he whispered, "Do you want that?"

Kate nodded, smiling slightly, and then looking down. Despite it all, her body still craved the hot kiss of leather. She still remembered the sweet, fierce joy of a whipping lovingly given and openly received.

Kevin loosened his tie, removing it. He started to unbutton his shirt, but she was there, her long, slender fingers nimbly slipping each button through its hole. She pulled the shirt open, touching her lips to his chest, kissing the dark blond curls as she moved her mouth down to his belly.

Kneeling, she unbuckled his pants, drawing the slim leather belt from the loops. She didn't go any further; it would be up to him. Instead she knelt, taking the whip in her hands, offering it, open palmed, to her lover.

Kevin took it, feeling the soft suede tresses, letting them glide through his fingers. If Kate noticed the slight tremor in his fingers, she didn't acknowledge it. She knelt, head touching the ground so that her hair fell across his feet. Her lovely bottom was offered up, waiting for the kiss of his lash. Kevin walked around behind her, holding the whip in one hand. He dragged it slowly across her bare back. Kate shivered slightly but stayed in position. Kevin drew back the whip and let it land with a splash of leathery sound against her soft flesh.

Kate drew in a breath. He struck her again, harder, and Kate sighed. Her body remembered the whip, loved it, wanted it. Kevin got into his own rhythm, loving the sound of leather against skin, watching her fair skin turn from creamy peach to dark pink. When his cock could no longer stand the strain, he opened his pants, pulling them down and kicking them away, along with his underwear.

Right there in the hall, Kevin crouched behind the panting girl and pressed his erect cock against her entrance and felt it slick and ready for him. Entering her, his cock sheathed in her almost virginal velvet tightness, he sighed. "Oh, Katie," he breathed, his heart full. "Oh, my love."

Kate arched back into him. "Fuck me! Oh please, fuck me!" Primal need turned Kate into a wild thing. There was nothing she would not do for her lover at that moment. Kevin grabbed Kate's hips, bucking into her, using her, lost in her. They fell together, collapsing to the ground, Kevin's briefcase and clothing discarded, forgotten. They lay still for some minutes, neither one thinking of Mark.

Chapter Seven

Kate was in the devil's chair. He wouldn't steal it from them. They were reclaiming their lives. And the lovely irony was that now they cherished what they shared, and truly appreciated that what they had was a gift, not a right.

Thick bands of shiny black leather bound her above the breasts, over the wrists and at the thigh and ankle. Kevin knelt at Kate's feet, his mouth buried in her sweet pussy. Her thighs were marked where he had just whipped her, and the heat of the whipping had aroused her to a fever pitch, which was turning to frenzy as he kissed and teased her.

Quickly releasing her bonds, Kevin lifted his angel from the chair and lay her gently on the soft carpet. "Who do you belong to?" he asked, his voice low.

"You! Always and only you," she whispered back.

Lifting himself over her, holding his body away from hers with his strong arms, Kevin slowly entered her, their bodies touching only at the genitals. She was wet and open for him, taking him in her velvet, hot tunnel, moaning a little as he filled her. Kevin eased down onto her, lifting her arms high above her head, pinning her by the wrists, claiming her completely.

They made love in slow motion, and it felt to Kate as if the world had stopped. The last vestiges of the nightmare that had been Mark fell away from her, lost in the swirl of delicious orgasm that left her almost unconscious. As she came to herself, she felt a little drop of water splash her face. A tear?

Her eyes opened and she looked up at her big, strong lover. A second tear rolled down his cheek and landed with a plop on her chin. "Kevin?"

He nestled his face in her neck, wrapping his naked body around hers. "Don't worry, my love," he assured her. "I'm just so happy. So sorry for what happened, but so joyous that we have each other." He grinned through his tears, and laughing, promising, "They're tears of joy."

Jewel Thief

Chapter One

Elena took a sip of the dry champagne that had just been poured for her into a fine crystal flute. As she listened to her date prattle on about the attendees at the party, she scoped out the room.

It reeked of money. Old money and lots of it—with fine antique furnishings set tastefully amid hand-stitched Oriental rugs and flanked by walls adorned with turn-of-the-century Impressionist masterpieces. Originals, she was pretty sure, or else damn good imitations.

The room was full of the rich and the beautiful. Elena didn't know any of them and yet she didn't feel out of place. She knew she exuded a certain elegance and confidence, even if she still sometimes felt like a kid inside.

"That guy there, he's got more power in his left pinky than half the people in here. And for this crowd that's saying a lot." Elena's eyes followed Roger's chin, with which he was attempting to discreetly indicate the man in question.

The fellow he was focused on wasn't much to look at—short and pudgy with a shock of gray hair over a kindly face. Perhaps anticipating her lukewarm response Roger added, "He's a judge in the fourth precinct. Mafia territory. Has himself a very nice house where he keeps his very nice money, courtesy of the folks who have greased his way along the path to blind justice."

Roger himself was a successful attorney who managed to deal with criminals without stepping on the wrong side of the law, at least not too far over to get caught. Elena didn't know him well and had no particular desire to know him better. He was good-looking enough, in a smarmy, oily kind of way, but definitely not her type.

What he was — was an entry into this house, where the jewels were kept. He was the foot in the door that her friend James, criminal accomplice and occasional lover, had provided her. James knew all the "movers and shakers" and used his connections to advantage. Elena had allowed Roger to presume this was a date, set up by their mutual friend James. Roger, recently divorced and hot on the trail, had seemed delighted when he'd arrived at her door, bouquet in hand, to greet his blind date.

Elena was after all quite the package, tall and slim with thirty-six C breasts that needed no artificial augmentation, and legs strong and lean from a lifelong habit of jogging three miles every morning at sunrise. Her head of thick, straight dark hair didn't hurt either, falling in shimmering waves that offset her gray-green eyes and full red lips.

People were always telling her she should be a model. But Elena didn't want to work that hard. She wanted to be rich — filthy rich, but she didn't want to get there "the old-fashioned way". No, she didn't want to earn it — she wanted to steal it.

Elena was a thief.

A careful, clever thief on her way to her first million with no intention of stopping there. At twenty-seven, she had grown tired of working for a living and had decided to do something about it. Her looks and her natural ease among the very rich had gained her entry into many of the finest homes in Westchester County. She had started small, snatching a few precious pieces of jewelry from bedrooms on her way to the upstairs bathroom.

Gaining confidence and some skills at the hands of her partner James, Elena learned to scope a room, to find the safe, to get it open and make her getaway. Alarm systems were still beyond her ability to disable, but James was handy with electronics and he was the one to get her in the door. Once she was in, it was up to her.

So far, they'd made five successful burglaries over the space of twelve months, two in New York, one in Connecticut and two in Massachusetts. None of the cases had been cracked. She'd never even been questioned. No one thought to suspect the lovely brunette who just happened to have been to each of the homes as a guest, or friend of a friend.

"That's the host. John London. Big investment banker. I'll introduce you if you like." Roger smiled importantly and put his hand proprietarily on Elena's arm. She resisted the urge to shake him off.

"That would be wonderful. I'd love to meet him."

Roger guided his date over to the little group of people standing around the host. He was tall, with golden blond hair falling over his forehead, drawing the attention to his bright blue eyes and craggy good looks. He looked careworn, not from age, but from a life lived fully—with grooves and lines that showed humor and passion. Elena judged him to be about forty, though his body still looked hard and strong under an elegant, tailored silk suit.

His reputation as a playboy preceded him. He was, she had to admit, extremely good-looking. She had come to the party with a preconceived notion that the host was probably a conceit and a fool who thought he could bed any woman he chose, simply because he was rich and handsome.

She hadn't been prepared for the actual man. It wasn't simply his good looks—there was something magnetic about him. Something compelling, even dangerous, that arrested her so that she found herself staring at him and had to force herself to turn her head away.

She wasn't the only one. The little group of men and women, mostly women she noted, all seemed to be focused on him as he held forth of some esoteric topic or other. The women seemed ripe somehow, their lips moistened, their eyes shining, as if he promised a taste of something secret and exotic and just for them.

His eye fell on her as she observed the scene and a dimple appeared in his left cheek as he grinned at her. Despite her better judgment, Elena felt a little flip-flop in her belly, as if she was some kid in high school and the captain of the football team had just noticed her.

The crowd seemed to melt away as the man approached Roger and Elena. Roger extended his hand, forcing the host to take it, though his eyes still lingered on Elena. "Roger. Roger Clement. You remember—we met at the Winston buyout. So kind of you to invite me tonight."

The host looked directly at Roger and smiled, remarking, "Yes, of course, I remember. Daltry and Smith, right? Your firm's counsel was invaluable in closing that deal."

As Roger stood beaming, the host looked Elena over, his eyes passing over her body in such a way that she had to resist a sudden impulse to shield herself from his gaze. His expression was confident, insolent and somehow sexual. Absurdly, Elena felt a hot blush on her cheeks. She turned away.

Roger, perhaps discomfited by the silent drama unfolding before him added, "And this is Elena. Elena Beckett. My date." If he put a slight emphasis on the word "my", it was understandable.

"London. John London. Jack to my friends." Jack extended his hand, smiling as Elena put hers into his. He shook it firmly, but without too much pressure. Elena couldn't stand it when men offered a limp-fish grip just because you were a woman. She smiled back.

"Like the writer?" Elena offered.

"Yes, though most people these days have never heard of him! Do you read?"

"Voraciously," Elena answered honestly, adding, "A pleasure to meet you. What a lovely home you have."

"Thank you. I like it. Though I'm thinking of moving out some of this clutter. I inherited it last year when my mother passed away, and I haven't done much with it since. Haven't had much time, to tell you the truth. But I'm going to get to it. Make it my own, you know."

"Well, your mother had excellent taste, nonetheless." Elena smiled, and glanced around the room. The safe wasn't in here. No. It was probably in the study. Wherever that was. If only she could ditch Roger and cozy up to Jack here, she could find out in a hurry. As it was, she'd just have to do a little snooping on her own.

The three of them talked for a few minutes about their mutual acquaintances. Several other people joined them and after a while, it wasn't too difficult for Elena to excuse herself to "find the powder room". Jack gestured in the direction of the little restroom near the front door while Roger admonished her to "hurry back, darling".

Trying not to wince, Elena nodded and smiled as she left the group. However, her return was a little less than direct. Instead of turning right and coming back to the living room, Elena turned left, quickly opening doors along the long hallway. She found the room she thought she was looking for—a den or study, with floor-to-ceiling bookshelves and a large, old desk in the corner. Throw rugs brightly adorned the hardwood floor. It was the kind of room men liked to claim as their own away from the womenfolk. It was also the kind of room, she had found, where men kept their toys and gadgets, including sexy things like safes hidden in walls.

James had done a little research beforehand and had determined that Jack London did in fact have a safe in his home. In fact, they had specially chosen him as their next heist because of it. MasterKey Safes & Locks had installed the safe, just this past year, presumably to keep things of value locked away. James' connection at MasterKey had come in very handy in three of their robberies and he had been paid handsomely for his troubles.

Quickly, Elena moved behind the desk, pushing aside the large oil painting—nothing but bare wall back there. She stood back, looking around the room, but the rest of the walls were covered with bookshelves. Where could it be?

She sat in the large chair behind the desk for a moment, pondering. As she sat, she tapped her foot impatiently against the floor. What was that? The floor sounded different just there—a sort of hollow sound. Kneeling quickly, she felt along one of the boards, searching for a hidden spring. Why not a floor safe?

She didn't find any springs, but she did find what she was looking for. A little metal ring was imbedded in one of the boards and when she pulled it up, a one-foot-by-one-foot section of flooring lifted up on silent hinges.

There it was! The MasterKey safe, promising precious delights just waiting for Elena to pluck for herself! She felt an almost sexual thrill as she contemplated the jewels and coins no doubt hidden within.

Glancing at her watch, she knew she mustn't tarry any longer. Quickly pressing the little door back into the flooring, she stood and smoothed her long red gown against her body.

With a last glance around the room, she slipped out and back into the noisy living room where champagne had dutifully done its work and inhibitions were effectively being lowered. "There you are!" Roger called, waving toward her. She gave a small return wave of greeting and walked over to him.

For her, the evening was done. She was dying to call James and tell him she'd found it! James and his contact had a list of all the combinations of all the safes installed by MasterKey.

This job was going to be a piece of cake.

Chapter Two

Two weeks had passed and Elena had managed to put Roger off enough so that he got the idea and faded away. Surprisingly, Elena had found herself thinking about Jack London—his handsome head of tousled blond hair and the way he threw back his head when he laughed. She found herself wondering if he was a good lover. She hadn't noticed any women on his arm at the party, though certainly several had hovered, laughing and hanging on his every word all evening. She knew he wasn't married.

This wasn't good. She didn't want to be thinking this way about the man she was going to rob. Though she didn't have much of a conscience when it came to stealing from the abstract rich, she had never been attracted to any of her other "victims".

James and his MasterKey contact had been busy with their end of the heist. These behind the scenes maneuvering were just as important, if not more so, than the actual break-in, and Elena knew and appreciated this. Though she was a thief, she believed in honor among her kind and wouldn't hesitate to share equally in whatever she managed to snare.

The date was set for this coming Tuesday. Jack London was scheduled to be down in the city attending a gala affair honoring the mayor.

If James played his cards properly, Elena would have twenty minutes from when he deactivated the system to when the alarm company was alerted. Armed with the combination and already familiar with the house, she didn't anticipate any problems.

Nevertheless, when the evening came, Elena felt the usual jittering of nerves. While she did get a real thrill from the whole scene, imagining herself as a sort of criminal Emma Peel, the fear in the pit of her stomach was also very real.

"Keeps you on your toes," James had offered as he knelt in the dark of the back door, fiddling with the electronic lock with some complex little tools. "You get complacent, you get caught. There—the door's open. The alarm's disabled. Go!"

As he faded into the dark, Elena slipped into the house. London's staff did not live in and the place was quiet. The kitchen light was on, shining into the darkened living room. Quickly she edged her way toward the hall where the study was. The door was ajar and she slipped in, flicking on her little pencil flashlight as she knelt by the floorboards that hid the treasure.

She had memorized the combination and she squatted now in her black spandex pants, twirling the little metal dial—twenty-two, forty-eight, thirty-nine. The latex gloves felt hot on her hands, but of course, it wouldn't do to leave prints. Slowly she slid the dial to its appointed spot. Something didn't feel right. She couldn't feel the tumblers falling into place.

A tiny edge of panic cut its way across her smooth demeanor. *Slow down. Try again.* Carefully she turned the dial, once to the left, two times around to the right, back again to the left. Shit! James' connection had messed up! This wasn't right.

Taking a deep breath, she tried a third time. She was so absorbed in what she was doing that she didn't hear a sound until suddenly…

"Well, well, well. What have we here?"

Time stopped.

It just froze as realization dripped over her like an icy shroud. Something was terribly wrong. Jack London was in New York City, but in the dim light reflected from the other room, Elena could make out a man who looked exactly like him, dressed in a tuxedo, a frown on his face, a gun in his hand.

Where was James? Why hadn't he warned her? It was his job to keep watch and call her via walkie-talkie phone. Instinctively, Elena's hand went to her phone to check if it was on. "Not so fast," Jack shouted. "Put your hands in the air or I'll blow your head off. You're in my house, and I promise I won't hesitate to shoot if you reach for that gun."

Gun? What? "It's a phone," she managed to say. "Not a gun." As Elena lifted her head, Jack flicked on the overhead light.

"Jesus H. Christ," he said softly. "I thought I recognized that voice. You're the lovely woman who was at my party with that idiot Clement!" His expression—at first incredulous, now darkened again. "What the hell are you doing here with your hands on my safe? What's going on? Spill it!"

Elena licked her lips. He'd called her a "lovely woman". Maybe she could use his apparent attraction toward her to wriggle her way out of this somehow. "Gosh, Jack. It was just a lark. A joke. You know, a bet…"

She trailed off as Jack's countenance darkened. "Save the bullshit stories for your idiot boyfriend. As far as I can see, you're guilty of breaking and entering and were in the process of attempting to steal my possessions. Felonies that will land you in prison for the rest of your natural life."

Elena had meant to hang tough. She could talk her way out of just about anything. But those words got to her. *Felony. Prison. Life.* Up until now, it really *had* been a lark, albeit a very profitable one. She'd gotten away so easy each time that this time, she had been too cocky, too sure of herself.

"You'd never have gotten into that thing anyway. I have a very special combination. No one knows it but me. I had it specially altered after I bought it. The items in there are too valuable to trust some third party with my combination.

"Now, little lady..." He gestured with the gun. "Stand up nice and slow and keep your hands over your head. A quick call to the police will get you out of my hair. I've got a splitting headache from a ridiculous day of negotiations. That's why I gave the dinner party, which you no doubt knew I was supposed to be attending, a miss."

Police. Life in prison.

Elena stood slowly, a peculiar ringing sounding in her ears. She felt nauseated and dizzy. The ringing got louder and she felt saliva gush in her mouth as if she was about to vomit. When her head struck the side of the desk, she didn't feel a thing.

"You fainted. Whoa, hold still. That blood is everywhere." Jack was holding a handkerchief to Elena's forehead. She opened her eyes, for the moment completely unaware of where she was. Then it all rushed back with sickening clarity as she stared into the concerned eyes of her captor.

"Listen, I've been thinking. Elena, right?" As she nodded, her eyes wide on him, Jack continued, "You've got a choice right now. You can either watch while I call the police…" *He hadn't called them yet! There was hope!* "…or you can call off your accomplices and listen to my proposal. It's what I do for a living, you know. Come up with alternate proposals—ways of looking at things no one else has thought of. It's made me a rich man."

Elena didn't speak. She licked her lips and tried to swallow. She was longing for a glass of water. To buy time she slowly peeled the now useless gloves from her hands, dropping them beside her.

"So?" he probed. "What'll it be?"

"I'm sorry," Elena answered. "I feel so dizzy. Thirsty. I'm not sure what you're saying." She had a pretty good idea, of course. He was going to blackmail her into giving her body to him for as long as he wanted it, in exchange for not calling the police. But he would always have it hanging over her. For as long as he wanted, he could threaten to turn her in. He was probably so well-connected he could get the book thrown at her even though breaking and entering was all she'd succeeded in doing.

Jack answered, "There'll be time for water, my dear. And plenty more. For right now, I'm going to make you an offer. And yes, you can refuse it. But you'll pay the price— the price you've earned by being a thief.

"Here it is, in a nutshell. Listen carefully, because I'm not in the habit of repeating myself. Not to be vain, but I can get any woman I want. I don't know if it's my looks or my money and frankly I don't care. You're beautiful, anyone can see that. But that's not what attracts me to you, or at least it's certainly not the only thing. You're feisty. You've got nerve, breaking in here the way you did. And you've read Jack London," he grinned.

"I'll be blunt with you. I like submissive women. I'm into BDSM. Bondage, discipline and sadomasochism. It's an orientation, a predilection—call it what you will. It pleases me to have my lover submit to whatever I ask, whatever I *demand*." He caressed the last word and Elena shivered, though without real understanding.

Warming to his subject as if he were chatting with a friend instead of holding a woman with a bleeding forehead, he went on. "Now, submissive doesn't equal passive. In fact, a true sub is stronger than any Dom, at least I think so."

He paused, fingering his chin with two fingers and said, "Here's my proposal for your consideration. I'm a busy man. I don't have a lot of time to cultivate relationships, but I do enjoy a good session with a good sub. One week. You will give me one week out of your life, and then you never have to see me again. During that one week, you will be my sex slave. You will obey my every command and wish, no matter how bizarre." Holding up a hand, he added, "Don't worry, I won't cause you any harm, nothing you can't handle at any rate. At the end of the week, you are free to go. This whole felony thing will be forgotten."

Elena stared at him. She was having trouble getting a handle on what he was saying. Yes, she had expected to give sex in exchange for her freedom, but bondage and discipline? Was the man out of his mind? Was he some kind of sick bastard who got off on torturing his sex partners? She shuddered and said, "Torture or prison? These are my options?"

"It's not torture. BDSM sex can be the most exciting and rewarding experience for both the Dom *and* the sub. There are people who would pay thousands for what I'm going to give to you, if you let me. I'm not going to keep you here against your will. *I'm* not a criminal. But if you stay, and we'll work up a nice agreement that is legally binding and releases us both from all liability, then you will belong to me, completely and utterly, for that time period."

The phone rang and Elena jumped. Jack reached to answer it. "It's the alarm company. Do I have a yes?"

Elena, knowing she had no choice, slowly nodded.

Chapter Three

The water streamed over Elena's head as she tried to clear her mind. The shower was one of those fancy jobs with jet sprays coming at you from all directions. As the hot water massaged her, she thought about how easily James had faded away with her phone call.

"James," she'd said, trying to keep her voice from trembling. "Listen, there's been a complication. London came back here. How he slipped by you, I don't know." When James started to interrupt, to defend himself from her implied reproach, she cut him off. "Stop. I don't have time. The thing is, he didn't catch me doing anything except standing in his kitchen, calling his name. I'm in his bathroom now. He bought the story that I had lost an earring and had come around looking for it and found the door open. He thinks *I* scared off some burglars and he's all thankful. I only have a second—I'm 'powdering my nose'. Listen—just make yourself scarce. I'll be in touch. We botched this one, but we're okay. I'll call you when things settle down. Bye now."

She clicked off her phone to Jack's slow applause. He was grinning as he said, "Well done. Well done. Quite the little actress, aren't you? I almost believed your little story, and let's hope he did, too."

"How *did* you get by him? He was supposed to warn me."

"I was on foot. There's a train station not half a mile from here. I often walk home. I like the exercise. He was probably posted by the driveway. You and your accomplice didn't do your research so well, did you?"

Elena hung her head. Though it was no longer bleeding, the cut on her forehead was throbbing gently and her head was pounding. Ironically, Jack said, "Hey, I guess you're good for me. That headache I had is completely gone! Maybe I get off on gorgeous criminals breaking into my house. And now I have you! For a solid week, you are going to serve me, slave girl. Aren't you." It wasn't a question—it was a statement of fact. An insolent sensuality fairly exuded from the man.

Elena stared at him, ignoring the sudden hot pulse at her sex. Thoughts of taking him down passed swiftly through her head. But even if he hadn't had a gun, he was easily eighty pounds of solid muscle heavier than she. What was a week, compared to ten to life in prison? She nodded as she lifted her hands to her temples.

"A nice hot shower should help, and a snifter of brandy. I'll get the brandy—you'll find everything you need in the guest bedroom shower. It's the second door on the right up the stairs. Allow me to escort you."

Now as she stood under the hot spray soaking up the heat she wondered what was in store for her. Jack was a seriously good-looking man but she wasn't used to being at anyone's mercy. In every relationship, she had always been the one in control, the one who called the shots. Not that this was a relationship, for God's sake. She didn't know what the heck it was.

She found she couldn't think clearly though the shower had helped to dispel some of the blind panic. At least she was still here, not being carted off in cuffs in a squad car.

As she was drying off with the large, thick yellow towel she had found hanging near the shower stall, Jack entered the bathroom, causing Elena to startle and try to cover herself.

"Very nice," he said, openly admiring her barely covered form. He was holding two large snifters of brandy, the amber liquid swirling at the bottom of each. He held one out toward her.

"Do you mind?" she said imperiously, forgetting for a moment her situation.

"I do, yes. Do you forget so soon that you belong to me? You can always renege, and I can always call the police. I don't think you want that though, do you? Now prove it and drop the towel."

Elena stared at him as if her facility for English had suddenly left her.

Jack set the snifters of brandy down on the bathroom counter and leaned up against it. "Must I repeat myself?" His voice was low, his smile dangerous.

Slowly she dropped it, revealing her long, firm body, the skin moist and smooth. Her rounded breasts were capped with gumdrop nipples of dark pink, which stood at attention in the damp air. She started to cover herself with her arms when Jack ordered, "Hands at your sides. I want to look at you."

She dropped her arms as he approached her. Reaching out to touch her forehead, he said gently, "There, that's not too bad. Just a superficial cut. It should heal quickly." His finger moved down, tracing her cheekbone, moving down her neck to her breast. He touched her nipple and she shivered.

Despite herself, her body was reacting to him. There was such a powerful quality about him—a masculine confidence that he had the right to do what he was doing. "Lovely," he murmured and then, "Kneel down. Right there, kneel for me."

He pushed her shoulder as he spoke, forcing her to her knees. Elena knelt, instinctively bowing her head. Leaning down, Jack lifted her chin, forcing her to look up at him. "You're lovely, Elena. From the first time I saw you, I was attracted to you. Is this really such a horrible punishment? To submit to me? No, don't answer right now. I can see you're still in shock. Whatever dangerous, silly games you've been playing—breaking and entering— I'm guessing you've been getting away with it. I'm guessing you had some kind of crazy idea that you and your buddy were invincible, that you'd never get caught.

"Now the game's up and you're cornered, like a rat in a cage. I don't want a rat, you know. I don't want you paralyzed from fear. It'd take all the fun out of it. I want, and indeed demand, complete submission. But submission is about strength and grace, as I hope to teach you."

He smoothed the wet hair back from her face and took the fallen towel, wrapping it gently around her shoulders. Taking one of the snifters from the counter, he handed it to Elena. This time she took it, swallowing the strong brandy in one gulp.

He drank his as well, after raising it in a silent salute to his captive. "Get up. Come to bed. You can sleep in the guest bedroom tonight. Your, uh, duties, won't begin until tomorrow. I imagine you've had all the excitement you can tolerate this evening. And I'll draw up a contract to set your mind at rest that I don't intend to hold you hostage, at least past this one week."

Still dazed, but grateful for at least this temporary reprieve, Elena accepted his offered hand and rose slowly, clutching her towel ineffectually against her naked body. The brandy was already doing its work as she felt it burning smoothly down her chest.

She had expected to toss and turn once she'd laid down on the bed. Jack, no doubt anticipating thoughts of escape, had informed her that the house was fully secure. He had reset the alarm system. No one could now get in and she could not get out.

It was almost a relief to realize she couldn't escape. She was just too tired and sore to contemplate it now, even if that was what Emma Peel would have done.

Morning came into her window with a blaze of sunlight. For a fraction of a second, Elena didn't know where she was. She heard classical music coming from outside of her room. As she sat up she heard whistling, Jack's presumably. She peed and washed her face in the bathroom, and then looked about for her clothing. They were nowhere to be seen. Not even her underwear.

She stepped back into the bedroom and opened the bureau drawers and closet. Nothing. "Uh, Jack? Mr. London?" She wasn't sure what to call him now that she was his "prisoner" in this bizarre arrangement. "Excuse me? My clothes?"

"Ah, good morning, sleepyhead." Jack was suddenly at her door, a glass of juice in his hand. "I was wondering if you'd ever wake up." He watched with apparent amusement as she scrambled toward the bed, jumping in and pulling the sheets around herself in a display of modesty.

"Your clothes. You won't be needing them, my dear. Not for the next week. Have you forgotten already? Sex slaves don't wear clothes, silly girl. At least not black turtlenecks and slacks. No, I think I'll keep you naked, at least for the time being. You have such a lovely form—it'd be a shame to hide it."

He smiled slowly, his grin curling up like a serpent as his eyes bore into hers. Less playfully, he said, "Now stand up, slave girl. Each morning you will stand by your bed for inspection while I decide what to do with you. Go on, up, up!"

Elena wanted to refuse. How dare this man, this bastard, command her to stand up for "inspection"! Yet, she believed he would honor his threat to turn her in and so—reluctantly—she stood naked by the bed, wrapping her arms around her body.

"No, no. Lesson number one—inspection position is hands behind your neck, fingers locked, legs spread." She blushed and bit her lip as he approached her, pushing her ankles apart with the tip of his bare foot. Jack was wearing black denim jeans and a royal blue T-shirt that exactly matched his eyes and set off his honey-blond hair. She realized he looked as good in these casual clothes as in the finely tailored tuxedo he had been in the night before. She wondered for a split second what he would look like naked, all long, lean muscles and broad chest. Internally, she chastised herself for these thoughts—this man was the enemy!

He stayed close and she could smell his cologne, something subtle and pleasing with a hint of sandalwood. A flashing desire to kiss his sensual mouth zipped through her before it was swallowed in her own outrage at her predicament. She assumed the "position"—what choice had she?

Jack stood back and took a long drink from his orange juice as he eyed her. "Very nice. Lovely in fact. I'd like to have you sitting at my feet while I eat breakfast. Are you hungry, Elena?"

His question made her realize that she was indeed. She smelled bacon and something with cinnamon wafting from the kitchen and her stomach growled. She nodded. "Lesson two," Jack said. "When I ask you a direct question, you answer with words, that is, if you are in a position to do so. And you use the address 'sir'. Am I clear?"

Elena stared at him, a crazy defiance rising in her, all the more ridiculous since she was standing there like some kind of peculiar, naked army cadet with her hands dutifully locked behind her head. "This is nuts," she began but he cut her off.

"Uh-uh, no, no. That won't do. This is your one warning, Elena. After this, each infraction will be met with punishment. I will decide the intensity of the punishment, based on the transgression. Now, let's try again. Are you hungry?"

"Yes, sir," she muttered, the words spit from her mouth like cherry pits.

Jack didn't smile. "Part of submission is behaving with grace. Since we only have a week, you'll be getting a crash course. That means I'll be less patient with you than I'd be with a lover. Grace means answering politely, with a sweetness and sincerity that befits your station. Do you understand?"

"Not really," Elena said, and then added as his countenance darkened, "sir."

"Beware, little girl. You push and I'll push back." He softened his stern tone, adding, "But it's all right to admit when you don't understand something. You may ask why I am doing something. You may ask for permission to speak, and then you may express your concerns. However, don't fool yourself that ours will be a reciprocal relationship. You are not, and I repeat—not—my lover. You are my slave.

"That means you subjugate your will to mine. Granted, what we will have this week is not a voluntary exchange of power, which in my estimation is the most beautiful and loving expression of a D/s relationship. No, what we have is a game, but it will feel very real to us both, I should imagine. Indeed, it is real. The feelings you will experience—the fear, the pain, the pleasure, the loss of control—it will be perhaps the most real thing you have ever experienced."

Reaching out, Jack touched Elena's breast, cupping and lifting it as if she were a melon in the supermarket. She drew in her breath sharply through her nostrils, not daring to protest. *The fear, the pain, the pleasure, the loss of control...* The words reverberated in Elena's head and she began to breathe more rapidly, her heart beating a little tattoo against her chest.

Jack, unaware or at least unconcerned, went on. "Now, you say you don't understand. I presume you don't understand the concept of 'grace'. That's okay. You don't have to get it, yet. I'll teach you. Each act of submission, whether voluntary or not, will bring you one step closer to that state of submissive grace where your very reason for being becomes to serve and to please me in all things. Of course, I don't fool myself that that will happen to you over the course of the week, but perhaps you'll get a taste of the potential intensity of the offering."

Elena had no response—it was all mumbo jumbo as far as she was concerned—just an easy excuse to force a woman to do whatever he wanted. Not that she imagined Jack London had to do much forcing. She recalled the slavish looks of adoration on the faces of the women at his party. Slavish! Well, not she! Elena had always prided herself on her independence. Consciously she slowed her breathing, willing herself to remain calm. Yes, she would do what this bastard required of her to get his rocks off, but only because she had no choice.

Which reminded her… "The contract? You mentioned a contract last night?" There was no *way* she'd put up with more than a week of this shit!

The slap to her face was swift and hard. The sting took a moment to register and Elena gasped, dropping her hands from behind her head to cover the spot where he had hit her cheek.

"That was for breaking the rules—again. I warned you that you would be punished. Put your hands back in position—now!" He barked the last word, and she hastened to obey, unshed tears shining brightly in her eyes.

His voice more gentle, Jack said, "Now Elena, you're not a stupid woman. You really do need to pay attention. Now listen carefully."

He spoke slowly, as if to a dimwitted child. Elena felt herself bridling, the tears drying in anger. "If you wish to speak when I haven't asked you a direct question, you need to ask for permission. Like this, 'Excuse me, sir, may I speak?' *If* I say yes, then you can ask your question or speak your piece. You will address me as 'sir' at all times. Now, shall we try again?"

Elena was silent, trying to find the will to obey him. Her arms were tired and she got the distinct feeling he would keep her standing naked in this ridiculous position all day if that was what it took to get her to comply. Forcing herself to speak with what she hoped approximated submission, Elena said, "Excuse me, sir, may I speak?"

Jack smiled cruelly, and Elena had a sudden feeling he was going to deny her. She knew in that instant if that happened she would lose it and lunge toward him, pummeling him, scratching and biting "like a girl".

But Jack simply said, "Yes."

Okay, she wouldn't beat him to a pulp, yet. "Uh, sir, you had said last night that we'd have a contract. You promised this really was just for one week, and then we'd call it even…"

"I did indeed, and you will find that I'm a man of my word. In fact, while you were getting your beauty rest, I already drew it up. I'll show you after breakfast. We can both sign. I made two copies. Believe me, after this week, I'll be just as culpable as you. It'll be in both our interests to have those contracts signed."

This made sense to Elena, and for the first time since she'd looked up and seen him standing over her in the study the night before, a few tendrils of the tight strings of fear in her gut eased themselves just a little.

"Anything else?"

"Uh, no, well, except you said something about breakfast? Uh, sir."

Jack laughed. "Not used to using that particular term of respect, eh? No, I don't guess you have to call much of anyone 'sir' to get what you want." He smiled a lecher's smile as his eyes raked her nude form. "Would you rather call me master?"

"No! Uh, sir."

"Well, good, because I despise the term. At any rate— breakfast. I was just about to sit down and eat. Why don't you come join me?"

He turned and walked out of the bedroom. After a moment's hesitation, Elena followed him, wishing she had at least a robe to wrap around herself. Once in the kitchen, Elena smelled the delicious cinnamon scent full-force. Jack opened the oven, removing a hot tray of freshly baked sweet rolls. He dumped them into a waiting breadbasket and set the basket on the table. The bacon he had draining on some paper towels, he now transferred to a platter and set on the table next to the steaming rolls.

As she stood uncertainly, he poured a cup of hot coffee into a waiting mug and added a bit of cream from a little pitcher shaped like a cow, its mouth the spout, its tail the handle.

Elena noticed he was only pouring the one cup, and there was only one place set at the table. She recalled his earlier comment— *I'd like to have you sitting at my feet while I eat breakfast.* Was that what this was about?

Her suspicions were confirmed as Jack turned toward her and said, "Right there. Kneel next to me, slave. Behave well, and I might give you a bite to eat. If you're very, very good."

Elena swallowed her outrage. Surely, this bastard didn't plan to starve her! The faint sting of his palm against her cheek coupled with the memory of his gun, no longer in view but surely nearby, reminded her that he meant business. The smell of the coffee made her actually sigh aloud, but she didn't want to give him the satisfaction of knowing how hungry she was. She knelt, dropping slowly to the floor.

"Ass on the rug. Sit cross-legged," he ordered matter-of-factly as he sat next to her in the chair, reaching for his coffee cup. She obeyed and became aware that her eyes were now exactly level with his crotch. He was turned toward her so that she couldn't help but stare at the bulge in his jeans, pressed provocatively against one strong thigh.

She swallowed, angry at her own body's betrayal as it responded to the closeness of his cock by sending blood to her nipples and clit. She shifted a little, not daring to move out of position but letting her eyes close.

Even this was forbidden apparently because Jack barked, "Open your eyes! Pay attention. You're a slave now and slaves must earn their food."

Elena's eyes flew open and she stared up at him. Her first estimation that this whole "slave" business was just a cover to have sex with her had been thoroughly shaken. What did this madman want of her?

"First of all, let's get those nipples nice and hard," he said, taking a sip from his steaming coffee mug. Elena licked her lips, trying not to salivate as she watched him. He went on, "Your breasts are large enough for you to do what I now propose. Let's see you suck those nipples. Get them hard and shiny wet for me with your mouth."

Elena's response was to stare at him openmouthed. Jack moved a bare foot, lifting it over her crossed legs and touching the toes to her pubic patch. Elena pulled back a little, though she didn't dare to push him away.

"Elena," Jack sighed, his voice weary. "This grows tedious. Am I going to have to whip you after each command? That can be arranged, but I was hoping you'd be able to demonstrate at least a modicum of obedience. The sooner you 'get with the program', the sooner you'll be rewarded. Being a sex slave isn't just about submission—there are sensual and other rewards as well. Little things, like getting to eat," he added sarcastically.

He took a bite from a sweet roll, licking a bit of icing from the corner of his mouth. "I've been more than patient. If you require a caning or a whipping to obey, I'll go get my toys."

"No!" Caning! Whipping! Did this stuff really exist outside of cheap porn novels? Evidently, it did but she didn't want to find out! Elena realized she had no choice. The bastard literally held her life in his hands. Her eyes on his, she lifted a breast and craned her head down, sticking out her tongue to make contact with her own nipple. It wasn't easy and she felt ridiculous doing it, but she was able to lick and wet it enough to make it erect. She did the same with the other nipple, annoyed at the heat she felt in her face. She didn't want to give him the satisfaction of seeing how embarrassed he made her. She sensed he would capitalize on that and humiliate her all the more.

"Good," he finally said, and she dropped her breasts with relief. "Care for a little coffee?" Jack held the mug down and she started to take it but he shook his head, "No, I'll hold it for you. I'll be feeding you, slave girl."

Elena bit back the retort, which rose to her lips, and waited passively for him to lower the cup to her lips. She sipped carefully. It was hot and delicious, just like she liked it with real cream and no sugar. He let her take several sips, and then said, "Ready to earn a bite of my famous sweet rolls?"

"Yes, sir," Elena managed. She really was starving she realized, and those rolls smelled so good!

"Rub your pussy for me. Then show me your fingers, all nice and wet. Make yourself hot for me, Elena."

"Oh, God. I can't. Not in front of you…" Elena had always been shy of touching herself in front of others, even though she didn't hesitate to take her own pleasure in the privacy of her own bedroom. How had he hit on the one thing that made her cringe?

"Suit yourself. Touch that sweet little cunt and show me your wet fingers, or wait until I'm done with my breakfast, at which time I'll cane you for your insolence and you'll wait until lunchtime to try again for a bite of food."

Shit. Shit, shit, shit. Even as she continued to hesitate, Elena knew she would obey him. What was the point of resisting? She was already naked and at his mercy. *Just get it over with*, she urged herself.

Slowly she reached down and touched herself. She stuck a finger inside of herself, trying to draw out the moisture fear was denying her. Jack watched her intently. His blue, blue eyes were fixed on her hand at her pussy, his sensual lips slightly parted. He hadn't shaved yet that morning, and his dark blond stubble made his lips look all the redder. He really was very good-looking. For the first time, Elena understood the term "magnetic" when applied to a person. Something about him drew her to him, despite herself, despite the situation.

She felt the sweet heat begin to mount inside of her and she moaned very slightly, her eyes still on his face. Jack shifted his legs a little, drawing her eye down his jeans. His cock was visible now, straining against the denim, snaking along his leg. He was clearly well-endowed and she flushed, looking away, her hand still buried in her own pussy.

"Let me see," he said huskily.

Elena hesitated for a fraction of a second, almost reluctant to stop. *Ridiculous!* She withdrew her hand and dutifully held up two shiny fingers, wet with her own arousal.

"Now lick them."

Her eyes locked on his, she slowly brought her fingers to her mouth. "Beautiful," he breathed. "Kneel up, sweetheart, you've earned your breakfast."

Obediently she knelt up, opening her mouth as he pulled a little piece from the cinnamon roll and held it out to her. Did danger heighten sensation? Was humiliation a stimulant to the appetite? Whatever the reason, as Elena chewed the hot, fresh bread she knew she had never tasted anything as delicious or perfect. Greedily she accepted every piece he offered her until the roll was devoured.

As he held the coffee mug again for her to drink, Jack laughed and said, "That's what I like—an appreciative slave. Liked it, eh?"

Elena nodded and then remembered to say, "Yes, sir."

"Brava," Jack said with delight. "Catching on at last. Would you like some more, my little piglet?"

Ignoring the gentle insult, Elena nodded. She could eat six more of those rolls, if he'd let her! Jack fed her patiently, gently wiping her mouth with his napkin and giving her sips of coffee every few bites.

She did polish off three more of them before Jack decided she had had enough. He stood and reached a hand down. "You've got potential, slave girl." He was grinning down at his captive as if they were old friends.

Elena felt a little thrill at his praise, which she quickly quashed, again annoyed at her positive response to a man she should despise. Still, she took his offered hand and stood slowly, unfolding her nude grace to Jack's appreciative gaze.

"You know, I was going to give you a good lesson in discipline and pain after breakfast, but you are so damn beautiful, I think I'm going to have to postpone my plans." Elena shivered at his words—*discipline and pain*! She tried to focus in on what he was saying. "I'm just going to have to fuck you first, Elena. You are so hot, I won't be able to concentrate otherwise."

He led her into his bedroom, which was as large as her whole apartment. A huge black-lacquer framed bed filled one wall, draped in gold-colored quilts and piled high with feather pillows also swathed in gold. Elena was nervous—the rape was at hand—and yet in a way she wasn't.

This at least was something she understood. Elena had traded her body for favors for as long as her curves had driven men wild with desire. Yes, this was a very peculiar situation, but at its bare bones not so different from other relationships where she had traded sex for something she valued. The stakes were just higher this time—her very freedom was in the balance.

Jack pointed to the bed and ordered, "On your hands and knees," as he pulled off his clothing. She started to twist her head around at the sound of his zipper opening, curious to see him naked though she wouldn't have admitted it. "Uh-uh," he admonished. "Turn your head back to the wall. Spread your legs and stay still, Elena. Take what's coming to you."

Elena tensed as he climbed onto the bed behind her. She wasn't sure what she was expecting, but when his tongue made contact with her pussy from behind, she jumped and exclaimed a little, "Oh!"

Jack grabbed her hips and held her still, his mouth again seeking her sex. His tongue was hot and smooth against her, skillfully awakening all her nerve endings with his kisses. Despite herself Elena moaned and pushed back slightly against his mouth.

Jack drew back and laughed softly. "So easy," he whispered. "The mark of a sub. Are you submissive, little girl? Am I only giving you what you never dared asked for?"

Elena didn't answer. She had barely heard him. Her body did want what he was offering, and she sighed with pleasure when his tongue again met the silky lips of her pussy. He brought her close, very close, to the edge before pulling away. She whimpered slightly, her mind shut down, her body focused on its pleasure and the sudden withdrawal.

She dared to look behind her and saw Jack leaning up, his long torso smoothly muscled, his large cock fully erect in his hand. *Oh, good*, she thought perversely, *he's going to fuck me now*. A part of her was amazed and angry at the rest of her for being such a slut—for capitulating so quickly as soon as his skillful mouth had aroused her. But the rest of her was pure sensation, eager for the promise of that thick, straight shaft filling her.

She turned back around, provocatively wiggling her bottom at him as she waited for the sweet invasion. He seemed to be taking his time — getting something from the night table next to the bed. A condom? He didn't know she was on the pill and she hadn't volunteered the information. How thoughtful to use protection, or was it that he didn't want to catch whatever disease he thought she might have?

The thought filled her with righteous indignation, but as she started to turn around again, he said, "No! Head to the wall. Forehead to the bed. Take what's coming to you, slut. It's nothing you don't richly deserve. You move out of position again and I'll have to spank you."

Dutifully she turned forward again, still aroused though the effect was somewhat dampened by his threats. She heard the telltale rip of a condom packet. At least she wouldn't get whatever diseases *he* had from all those girlfriends he probably had!

As the head of his cock pressed against her entrance, Elena sighed and pushed back ever so slightly, again eager for his invasion. He penetrated her, sliding in to the hilt and eliciting a grunt of pleasure from her. In and out he moved, his hands now caressing her sides, his head leaned over her so that she could feel his breath on her neck.

She felt his hand on her pussy, the fingers drawing her moisture along the folds of her sex. His hand was sure — he definitely knew what he was doing, unlike so many men who fumbled and were too rough or too gentle. He was perfect.

This was better than jail, she rationalized, but her body, without words, was signaling its joy as she felt a mounting orgasm rising against his fingers and cock. She couldn't help but revel in the delicious sensations as her blood coursed through her body, rushing to her sex in its impending release.

Suddenly she was empty—he had pulled out! The moment of orgasm was interrupted by his withdrawal and Elena moaned in frustration. This time she felt the cock head again, but not at her pussy! He was pressing against her ass!

She felt his hand against her face, stroking her hair. Gently, Jack said, "Slave, I am going to test your submission. Because of the unusual nature of our relationship—what with our one-week stipulation, I don't have the luxury of training you properly. Of teaching you about the searing pleasures of erotic submission in a slow and leisurely fashion. Unfortunately, for us both, you will be getting the 'crash course'.

"What I'm getting at here is that I'm going to fuck you in the ass, my sweet slave girl. I'm going to claim you in that most primal of ways and you are going to submit to it. With grace or not—that's up to you." As Jack spoke he continued to stroke Elena's hair, his touch sensual as he trailed his fingers down the back of her neck.

Not a virgin to anal sex, but never particularly caring for it, Elena protested weakly, "Please. I don't want it."

"Ah, but this isn't about what you want, is it, my love? You have absolutely no say in the matter. You lost your right to protest when you broke into my home and tried to plunder my belongings. Now you are paying the price. It will go so much better for you if you can accept the inevitable."

He leaned away from her for a moment, again taking something from the nightstand. Elena didn't dare turn around to see. Her heart was pounding in her ears, and she swayed slightly in her crouched position.

She felt him again behind her, his rigid cock again at her nether entrance. She realized, even as it stretched her painfully open, that his penis was liberally smeared with a lubricant. Elena tried to relax against the inevitable onslaught. She didn't dare to fight him, afraid his continued promises of a whipping would come to fruition, but the pending orgasm had definitely receded.

Slowly he eased his manhood into her ass. She found the pain lessening once the whole cock was inside of her. As Jack began to move against her, his fingers again found their mark. The pain in her ass eased as his fingers danced across her pussy, leaving spirals of pleasure in their wake. She found herself arching back against him. His cock actually felt *good* inside of her now, filling her most private orifice while his fingers made her cry out, "Yes, yes, yes!"

They came together, Jack collapsing gently against her as he pulled her down and onto her side, his cock still buried inside of her. "Lovely girl," he murmured, his strong arms wrapped tightly around her. Dreamily she lay still a moment. If she hadn't known better, she would have thought they were lovers instead of enemies in a very strange war.

Chapter Four

Elena stood stretched and taut in a room full of mirrors. She was standing in cruciform, her wrists and ankles shackled in well-worn leather cuffs that had obviously been used many times before.

Attached to the cuffs by metal clips were thick chains that were secured to large eyehooks in the ceiling and floor of what Jack had told her was his "playroom". At first glance, it looked like an exercise room, with mirrors along three of the walls and various pieces of equipment placed around the room. But in addition to the expected exercise bicycle and treadmill, there was a high, straight-backed chair with metal cuffs on the arms and legs, a long, low gynecological table complete with stirrups and an impressive array of whips and floggers hung against one wall.

The prisoner and her captor had actually fallen asleep together. To her surprise, Elena woke up slowly from sex-laden dreams, in which Jack figured prominently and romantically, to find his arms still wrapped around her. She wouldn't have minded him "taking" her again, but he had other plans.

"Come on, sleepyhead," he had said as he jumped up, giving a big stretch. "The mail will be here soon. I want you to read the contract so we can be done with that part of things. Then I'm going to introduce you to the potentials of masochistic pleasure."

Before he started the "session" as he called it, he had retrieved a bottle of cold water from a little refrigerator tucked into a corner of the room. Again, she was not permitted to feed herself, but was forced to open her mouth and let the water ease down her throat. It was wonderfully refreshing and she didn't even mind when a bit slipped down her chin and trickled onto her breast, a droplet glistening for a moment at her nipple.

Leaning down, Jack had kissed her mouth then, for the first time. His lips were cool and supple against hers, his tongue warm and insistent as he explored her mouth. His breath was sweet and she responded, in spite of herself, to his kiss. It was Jack who pulled away finally, smiling enigmatically as he watched her move forward slightly, seeking his mouth with hers for a fraction of a second before she mastered her emotions.

He had chained her to floor and ceiling, as she stood compliant and passive. She had told herself that she had no choice — this was her end of the deal and if she just took what he meted out for this one week, she was home free. She would never have to see Jack London again, and more importantly, she wouldn't be facing a prison term!

The contract had been straightforward — absolving her of all culpability once she had completed her week of "penance" at his hands. He'd sealed one copy, allowed her to address it to her apartment in the city and had handed the stamped envelope to the mailman while she hid discreetly behind the door as witness.

"Though it might not stand up in a court of law, this document would ruin me as surely as it would implicate you," Jack had promised as he'd signed each contract with a confident flourish. She had silently agreed, recognizing that as a prominent businessman, he had as much to lose as she did by going public with their bizarre arrangement.

In fact, actually getting caught had cured Elena in one fell swoop of her life of crime. She planned to go "on the straight and narrow" once she got out of this crazy place. She would move far away, leave the state altogether and start fresh somewhere new. She could always model or maybe go back to college and get that law degree she had sometimes thought of pursuing.

Though she'd been furious at being caught, hadn't *she* been the one trespassing—violating this man's home with intent to steal his most prized possessions? A new feeling for Elena—remorse—had slipped over her senses, making her almost want to apologize to this man who now held her captive. Almost—but not quite.

Her thoughts were jerked back to the present by Jack's sudden presence in front of her. He was holding a wooden paddle, like a ping-pong paddle, only made of a thick wood and varnished to a shiny finish.

"Ever been paddled, slave girl?"

"No, sir," she whispered, her eyes wide with fear. She felt so vulnerable cuffed and spread like this. She could see her image in the mirrors, multiplied a thousand-fold from one mirror to the next, bound and helpless in her chains.

Playfully Jack swatted her behind, making Elena jump. "What a great ass you have, slave. Perfect for fucking but even better for whipping." With his free hand, Jack cupped one cheek, lifting its sweet heft a little and letting it fall. Elena knew her ass was one of her best features but she was embarrassed nonetheless by his attentions, as she stood naked and exposed.

He swatted the other cheek, harder this time and Elena jerked forward and yelped. Despite the sting — perhaps because of it? — when he dropped a hand to her sex, he laughed a low, sensual laugh as he felt her wetness.

"You have potential," he said again. He smacked her several times, each one harder than the last, until Elena was panting, her breath coming fast.

"Please," she managed, "please…"

"Please what?" Jack said cruelly. "Please smack me again, sir? Please may I have another?" He punctuated his words by swatting her again, the sound reverberating in the room.

"Please! No more! No more, sir, no more." Elena was leaning hard against her bonds, a sheen of sweat covering her skin. Her ass was stinging, the flesh darkening to crimson in the mirror behind her.

Relenting, Jack dropped the paddle and stood behind her, pressing his body against hers. He was shirtless, his jeans hugging the low-slung hips of an athlete. The denim of his pants felt rough against her tender, abraded flesh. Reaching around her, he cupped her breasts and nuzzled her neck with his mouth.

Elena experienced a confusion of feelings. She could no longer pretend she wasn't deeply attracted to this man, in spite of his keeping her prisoner, in spite of the anal sex, the chains and cuffs, the paddling. When he kissed her neck, she felt his soft hair against her cheek. She couldn't help but sigh a little tremulous mewl of pleasure when the fingers of one hand rolled her nipple to full erection while the other hand strayed down to her wet and spread pussy. She knew she was supposed to hate this man — to keep up her defenses and simply "get through" this torture. Despite herself, she knew she was falling for him.

Could it be she was submissive, even masochistic, and had never had a clue? She didn't know. It was all too new and too bizarre. She didn't have time to ruminate on this though, as Jack again brought her to the edge of orgasm before pulling away, leaving her needy and wanton in her chains.

This time he produced a whip, a heavy flogger he removed from the wall as she watched with eyes as big as plates. He dragged its suede tresses along her back and ass, tickling her flesh with its softness.

"I'm going to whip you now, slave girl. Just flow with it, and you might surprise yourself. It can be the most sensual experience of your life if you let it be." He drew back and let the lash fall against her ass. It stung a little, though much less than the paddle.

He continued to whip her, gently at first, varying the tempo so she couldn't help but jump slightly each time skin and leather met. At first, she watched herself and him in the mirror, watched the leather strike her back or her ass or her thighs. Soon she dropped her head back, her hair streaming behind her in a burnished cascade, her eyes closing of their own accord.

It hurt, make no mistake about that. It stung more and more as her flesh became more sensitized and tender from the continued lashing. And yet, at the same time, something began to happen. Along with the pain came a strange, fierce pleasure. She took a perverse pride in her ability to "take a whipping" but something more than that was at play.

The heat in her skin actually transmuted somehow into a heat in her sex—a rising passion for the very man who was tormenting her. She began to murmur something, at first just a whirring sound that Jack mistook for her labored breathing.

Jack moved around her in a dominant lover's dance, alternating the lash for sensitive fingers that pulled Elena's passion from her almost against her will. The sound was louder until at last he understood her. "Yes, yes, yes," she was chanting, not even aware she was making a sound.

"Oh, God," Jack moaned, his eyes ablaze with lust as he whipped the now willing slave bound and chained and at his mercy. One final savage blow, and then he dropped the whip, released her cuffs and held her as she sank against him, her eyes still shut, her skin burning hot with a fever of passion.

When he made love to her there on the floor, it wasn't as Master and slave, as captor and prisoner. It was a lovers' embrace, as timeless as life itself and as sweet.

Chapter Five

Something had altered between them though neither openly acknowledged it. As the days passed, Jack continued to train his "slave girl", introducing her to the riding crop, hot wax, being bound and blindfolded, and sexually tortured without being permitted to orgasm. Or course, when she did anyway, she was soundly "punished".

Neither of them admitted the strange feelings blossoming silently between them. Jack continued to insist Elena address him only as "sir". He continued to inspect her each morning at bedside and to make her eat, kneeling at his feet, naked and dependent on his goodwill. He continued to take her "by force" when he wanted to fuck her and he continued to push her to new heights during "sessions" in his torture chamber.

Elena continued to tell herself she was only enduring it all in order to fulfill her end of the bargain and thus escape from the law. But her silent reproaches to herself as she took pleasure or was thrilled by whatever Jack was doing to her at the moment, became less and less frequent. Finally, she gave up even the pretense of internal resistance.

To her astonishment, she found she didn't *want* the week to end! This was crazy and she knew it. The man had essentially kidnapped her and held her against her will. No matter how sexy and desirable he might be, that single fact should have made her hate him!

Yet, instead of hatred, Elena found herself dreaming of him at night. She would awaken many times in the night and turn to stare at the man sleeping next to her. He had never let her go back to the guest bedroom after that first night, and she had found that she didn't want to.

In the repose of sleep, he looked so young and vulnerable. The cruel tilt of his waking smile was eased into a sweetness as he lay sleeping. His eyelashes, though light in color, were thick and impossibly long, casting a shadow against his cheek. She found herself feeling almost maternal toward him at these secret moments in the night. She found herself feeling something that felt like love. *Ridiculous!* But was it?

The last day arrived, and both Jack and Elena awoke out of sorts. Neither had spoken to the other about how to end this bizarre arrangement. At breakfast, Elena started to kneel at Jack's feet on the little rug he now kept for the purpose.

He surprised her by saying, "No. For today, sit here, next to me. I want to look at you."

She did as he commanded, not asking why. She felt odd sitting there as his "equal" after a week of kneeling at his feet. She wasn't sure if she was supposed to eat for herself or await his "feeding". He had already started eating—taking a helping of the ham and cheese omelet he had just slid from its hot, buttered pan to the serving plate. When he reached for a croissant, he stopped and looked at her.

"I'm sorry," he said. "Please, help yourself. Today is different. Today is the last day. You can feed yourself." Elena hesitated. This felt strange, after being fed these many days! And yet, how absurd. She'd fed herself all her life! It was about time he had let her join him at the table, as an equal.

As an equal. What did that mean, exactly? Could two people be equal in a D/s relationship? Hadn't he made it very clear at the beginning that they were in no way "equal"? What was it he had said precisely? As she bit into the hot egg and savored the melted cheese and salty ham, she recalled his words. *"Don't fool yourself that ours will be a reciprocal relationship. You are not my lover. You are my slave."*

Had this past week of intense experience been nothing more than a man getting his rocks off by practicing his particular fetish with a handy woman who'd fallen into his lap by strange circumstance? Did she mean nothing to him beyond a game of "Master and slave"? And what was this strange ache right in her chest? Could a heart actually *hurt*? All at once, what she'd been dancing around in her mind leaped to the forefront with a clarity that made her actually gasp aloud.

"What?" Jack asked, looking intently at the beautiful naked woman sitting across from him. There was a confident ease to her pose now, so different from the first day when she had felt like a terrified little rabbit caught in a wolf's lair. Would he be as graceful sitting naked, instead of in his silk pajamas as he was?

"Oh, nothing. I…that is…" Elena didn't dare confess what she had just realized. The man would laugh her out the door. "Nothing," she said again. "This omelet is delicious."

Jack watched her a minute more, but didn't press her. Instead, he said, "I'll be right back." When he returned, he was carrying his own terrycloth robe. "Here," he said, "You can put this on if you like. You look a little cold."

Elena took the offered robe and held it a moment, not sure what to do. It smelled nice, like Jack. She resisted a sudden urge to press it against her face and smooth her cheek against the fabric. *Ridiculous!*

"Don't you want to wear it?" Jack asked, watching her with a quizzical expression on his face.

Elena stood and slipped the robe on. It came down well below her knees and the three-quarter sleeves came almost to her wrists. How odd it felt to be clothed after a full week of being naked!

They finished the meal in silence, lingering over second cups of coffee. Jack read the paper or at least stared at it. Elena looked out the large bay window and marveled that she'd just spent the strangest week of her life with a man she'd been determined to hate but had to admit — she hesitated in her own mind, but the words slipped out of her mouth, betraying her — "loved him."

"Excuse me?" Jack looked up, distracted from his reading.

Elena turned away, feeling a hot blush creep along her neck.

He was quiet again, and then said only, "Elena." She heard the yearning in his voice. "This is hard. I didn't think it would be so hard."

"What?" Elena asked, glancing sidelong at him, her breath catching as she anticipated what he might say.

"You. Me. This whole thing ending. I know it was a horrible thing to do to you. To hold you prisoner like this. To presume that I had the right to 'teach you a lesson' for your 'sins'." He punctuated the words with little quotation marks in the air.

Elena didn't respond, waiting to see where this would lead. Jack continued, now looking into his coffee cup as if ashamed to face her. "I had no right, Elena. Yes, you broke into my house. I have no doubt you would've robbed me if you could have. But nonetheless, I had no right to do what I did."

He paused, looking out the window. "It really started out as a game." He put his hand over hers and she didn't pull away. "I thought I'd give you a day or two of some rough treatment. Shock you straight, if you will. Have some fun in the process. I had no idea we would connect like this. I figured, frankly, that you were too beautiful to be worth a damn."

As Elena started to protest this remark, not sure if she was annoyed or pleased, Jack held up a hand, laughing. "I know, I know. A very sexist thing to say or think. I guess I've had a couple of lousy experiences with women who were more focused on their own beauty than on any kind of meaningful relationship. I wasn't kidding when I said that a D/s relationship, when entered into lovingly and willingly by both parties, can be the most erotic, intense and rewarding experience on the face of the earth."

He paused, taking a deep breath and slowly expelling it. "But I took you by force, Elena. I took what should only be offered freely. I was a greedy bastard who saw an opportunity and grabbed it. Now instead of a possible loving relationship with the most exciting, loving woman I've ever met, all I get is one stolen week."

Elena stared at her "captor" and to her surprise saw tears in his eyes. She felt them spring into her own. "No," she said softly, not quite sure she could dare say what she longed to tell him. Somehow she found the courage because she added, "It doesn't have to end. If you don't it to. Sir."

She grinned with this last title and Jack laughed outright. "Trained you well, eh? A quick study for just one week. But seriously." Jack slipped out of his chair, dropping to one knee like a lover in some corny movie about to propose. He took Elena's hand in both of his and said, "If you'll give me another chance, Elena... If you'll let me start over with you. Not because you felt you had no choice, but because it's something we both want..." He paused, perhaps not daring to continue, not daring to hope.

"Yes," she whispered. "I want it, too."

Jack stayed kneeling a moment longer, as if frozen while he absorbed her answer.

He jumped up suddenly, laughing a huge full-throated guffaw of sheer joy. Pulling Elena up into his arms, he lifted her and spun around, making her laugh, too. Their laughter quieted after a moment, but still he held her tight in his arms. Slowly he dropped his head, nuzzling her neck with his nose.

Elena turned her face toward his and their lips met in a kiss. Slowly Jack moved with Elena still in his arms. He carried her to the bedroom, laying her gently on the bed. When he pulled the soft belt off the robe Elena was wearing, she didn't protest. A small smile curved her lips as he stared in open admiration at her naked, perfect form. She felt beautiful, sensual and desired. She felt no impulse to cover herself — let her lover take his fill.

Jack stood back, unbuttoning his pajama top and slipping the silky pants from his strongly muscled thighs. "I want you, Elena. I want you as my lover, as my submissive, as my sex slave, as my goddess. Do you want that?"

Elena nodded slowly, her eyes bright with anticipation as he lowered his strong body over hers, taking her wrists gently in his hands. As he lifted her arms over her head his lips found hers, his tongue entering her mouth as his shaft entered her sex.

She was eager for him. Being held down by her wrists, stretched now high over her head, only intensified her excitement as he moved his hips in such a way that the undulating pleasure was almost too much to bear.

Was she submissive? Was she masochistic? Who cared? What she was, was more aroused than she had ever been in her life. In a way, it was as if she had been sleeping through time, insensible to the possibility of intense feeling.

Jack, at first through force, but now through love, had made her come alive to the possibilities of a life truly lived, fully experienced. When they climaxed, tears rolled down Elena's cheeks but not from sorrow. In fact, her heart was singing its first tentative song of joy.

Later that morning when the two lovers awoke from their catnap, Jack turned to Elena in the bed and said, "Remember that safe you were trying to pillage, my little criminal? Come see what's in it."

Elena crouched near Jack as he twirled the little, heavy-metal dial of the floor safe. In a few seconds, he had it open. It was a least a foot deep and she watched him reach down, feeling for what he wanted.

He withdrew a soft, felt pouch of gray, tied at the top with string. After untying the string, Jack slid out the contents onto the desk. "I have other things in there—

papers and bonds and things I don't choose to trust to a bank—but this is what really counts for me. This was my mother's jewelry. The really precious pieces that she treasured all her life. Some of it has been in the family for generations."

As he spoke, Jack rifled through several little jewelry boxes until he found what he was looking for. "Ah," he said, holding up a pale blue ring box. "This is it." As Elena watched, Jack opened the little box and lifted the ring out of it.

It was the most beautiful thing she had ever seen—a single, large ruby flanked by a little circle of sapphires and diamonds set in platinum. It was beautifully made and hearkened back to old Europe—not flashy, but simply a work of art.

"Oh," she breathed admiringly. She truly was not expecting what happened next.

Again, her romantic darling—when had he become that?—knelt before her. He took her hand and slipped the ring on her finger. It looked as if it was meant for her hand, beautifully offset against her long, slender fingers.

As she started to protest he said, "Please. Accept this ring as a token of my abiding affection. Of my love for you. No," he cut off her attempt to speak. "Please, don't say anything. I have no right to ask anything more of you. This isn't an engagement ring—your acceptance of it binds you to nothing. I just want you to have it. I want you to enjoy it. It would make me happy to know you were wearing it, even if you leave today and I never see you again."

Elena couldn't control the bubble of laughter that now spilled out. As she held out her hand for him to stand up she said, "Oh, stop, you melodramatic idiot! I already said I wanted to stay! How could I go after what we've shared today? What do I have to do, beat you into submission?"

"Okay, okay," Jack laughed, too, standing. "I just wanted to make sure. I don't want to bully you ever again. Whip you and use you like the slave slut you are, yes, but no bullying."

Elena laughed again, understanding perfectly what he meant. She had discovered her submissive and masochistic nature this week, and she thrilled to his promise that that part of their "relationship" wouldn't have to end.

Standing on tiptoe, she pulled Jack's head down to hers and kissed him on the lips. "I love you, Jack London." As they stood locked in a lovers' embrace the ruby from Elena's ring shone richly against the back of Jack's neck where her hand rested. The thing she would have stolen was now hers, with no strings, given with love, a gleaming promise of things to come.

Enjoy this excerpt from
Sacred Circle
© Copyright Claire Thompson, 2005

Robert Dalton — Elder, Coven of the Red Covenant. It was neatly inscribed on one side of the card. On the other, in a thin angular scrawl he had written, *124 Charles Street. Saturday, 9:00 p.m.* Beneath it was a telephone number.

Grace fingered the little card. It was printed on fine, heavy stock, the lettering engraved in embossed shiny red. She was lying in her daybed, staring out the window. Her room was hot, despite the best efforts of the ceiling fan overhead. The little window-unit air conditioner in the adjoining room was wheezing its best effort to cool the place, but the tropical summer balm of New Orleans won out.

Grace sat in her panties and bra, her elegant black dress and high-heeled sandals tossed aside. Lifting her heavy French braid, she piled it on top of her head a moment, letting the wet breeze from her open window blow gently against her neck. The thick, waxy leaves of the magnolia tree outside her window were dripping with the recent rain shower. She'd just missed getting wet as she hurried home from the party, her mind reeling, her heart racing.

Why was she acting this way? It certainly wasn't Robert Dalton. While reasonably attractive — he was not her type. She preferred a more restrained sort of person. Someone more modest and less ostentatious.

No, it wasn't the man.

It was what he had offered.

She knew it was ridiculous. Why was she now suddenly allowing adolescent fantasies to run amuck in her head this way? She'd held such a tight rein for so long on feelings she had almost come to believe were nothing more than the feverish imagination of a young girl.

What had he said? "To spill a little of life's essence." Yes! That's what she felt now. A desperate longing for some of that promised "essence". Her own essence was flattened, she felt—a dried and sputtering spirit, left starving and hollow from years of denial and neglect. His one whisper of the chance for blood had set her body trembling, aching for it.

Yet, surely it was all a game? How could it be more? What was wrong with her? Had she read so many tomes about the creatures of the night that now she actually believed she was one? Ridiculous! Even if they did still exist, surely she would have known such a thing about herself. It would have manifested itself before now. Where were her fangs? The elongated canines reported in legend and exploited in Hollywood movies?

Parting her lips, gingerly she touched the pointed little teeth that could pierce skin and sinew with ease, if she were a real vampire. Lifting a thin white wrist, she bit gently against it, wondering what it would be like to actually puncture another's flesh. To pierce the vein and watch the glorious red tide flow from it, waiting for her special kiss. Was it her imagination, or did her canine teeth suddenly seem longer, sharper?

A bottle of wine stood next to her bed. A half-full bottle of cabernet sauvignon she'd grabbed from the kitchen counter on her way to her bed. She pulled out the cork and poured a glass. Lifting the glass goblet, she tilted her head back to take a long, deep drink, savoring its sweet burn.

Grace sighed, the image of a pale throat offered sliding unbidden into her consciousness, even as her fingers slipped down to her panties. She finished the glass and poured another, drinking it quickly. She realized she wanted to be drunk. To give herself permission in this way to do what she knew she was about to do.

So tight had been her own censorship of her true feelings that she rarely allowed herself the fantasy that was now stealthily easing its way into her brain. That pale throat, bared for her. Dark black hair curled in tendrils around it. The throat was strong, sinewy with corded muscle. It was a man's throat. Whose it was did not matter. It was an image that had floated through her dreams many times before.

Only now did she allow it to come through her conscious thought. She focused on it, imagining the face that would go with such a sensual and exposed throat. A strong jaw, a cruel mouth, but softened when it smiled. Lips ruby red, parting, revealing the elongated canines of her lover…

Her lover! Grace's fingers found their mark now, pushing aside the silky fabric of her panties. Her pussy was wet, eager for her touch. She rubbed and swirled in little arcs against her sex, moving toward the center and then away, wishing it was someone else's touch.

The wine coursed through her veins, giving her permission to explore the secret fantasy more fully. Recalling a half-forgotten dream, Grace closed her eyes. The dream brightened — its colors and feelings vivid in her mind's eye. It became more real than her narrow daybed in her small apartment, or her simple, rather dull life. For just that moment she didn't feel weak or in pain.

She could almost smell her lover now — the scent of exotic lemony spices and heat she'd experienced at the Vampire Ball. The lover of her dreams — with his dark hair and cruel smile.

They were naked, lying together on a large featherbed in the middle of a dark warm forest. He was leaning up on one elbow, kissing her hair, her forehead, her cheekbones, her lips. Slowly she felt his soft mouth edge down toward her throat.

Her golden auburn hair was loose around her head. She moved it herself, giving him access, desperate for what he was going to do. *Yes*, she thought now, *yes, do it. Take me. Claim me. I want it.* Grace moaned aloud as she rubbed herself, slipping a finger into her cunt as the dream image of her lover bit her neck, making her gasp.

He suckled at her throat, pressing his long body against hers. She shifted, her mouth watering, as she smelled her own blood on his lips. Silently she told him it was her turn, and he lay back, baring his own throat for her. She leaned over, dropping her head down, covering his face with her hair as she licked his supple flesh. In her fantasy she bit down, while in real life she only moaned, writhing against her own fingers, the sweet rusty taste of blood almost real to her.

As her sharp little teeth pierced the flesh, the impossibly rich red blood gushed like two little fountains of life against her mouth. She pulled back, trying to catch the flow, not wanting to waste a drop of his essence. It tasted better than anything she'd ever experienced in real life. It was more than drink, more than food. It went beyond mere sustenance. It was, quite literally, her life's blood.

Oh! It felt so real, just for that moment.

With a cry she came, jerking in uncontrollable little spasms, as her fingers drew out the last bit of pleasure. She fell on her side and her hand flew out to steady herself, knocking the bottle of wine from its perch, and onto her white sheets. The wine spread in a dark red pool. Grace didn't see—she was asleep, lost in blood-drenched dreams.

Why an electronic book?

We live in the Information Age—an exciting time in the history of human civilization in which technology rules supreme and continues to progress in leaps and bounds every minute of every hour of every day. For a multitude of reasons, more and more avid literary fans are opting to purchase e-books instead of paperbacks. The question to those not yet initiated to the world of electronic reading is simply: *why?*

1. *Price.* An electronic title at Ellora's Cave Publishing and Cerridwen Press runs anywhere from 40-75% less than the cover price of the <u>exact same title</u> in paperback format. Why? Cold mathematics. It is less expensive to publish an e-book than it is to publish a paperback, so the savings are passed along to the consumer.

2. *Space.* Running out of room to house your paperback books? That is one worry you will never have with electronic novels. For a low one-time cost, you can purchase a handheld computer designed specifically for e-reading purposes. Many e-readers are larger than the average handheld, giving you plenty of screen room. Better yet, hundreds of titles can be stored within your new library—a single microchip. (Please note that Ellora's Cave and Cerridwen Press does not endorse any specific brands. You can check our website at www.ellorascave.com or

www.cerridwenpress.com for customer recommendations we make available to new consumers.)

3. *Mobility*. Because your new library now consists of only a microchip, your entire cache of books can be taken with you wherever you go.

4. *Personal preferences are accounted for*. Are the words you are currently reading too small? Too large? Too...**ANNOYING**? Paperback books cannot be modified according to personal preferences, but e-books can.

5. *Instant gratification*. Is it the middle of the night and all the bookstores are closed? Are you tired of waiting days—sometimes weeks—for online and offline bookstores to ship the novels you bought? Ellora's Cave Publishing sells instantaneous downloads 24 hours a day, 7 days a week, 365 days a year. Our e-book delivery system is 100% automated, meaning your order is filled as soon as you pay for it.

Those are a few of the top reasons why electronic novels are displacing paperbacks for many an avid reader. As always, Ellora's Cave and Cerridwen Press welcomes your questions and comments. We invite you to email us at service@ellorascave.com, service@cerridwenpress.com or write to us directly at: 1056 Home Ave. Akron OH 44310-3502.